★

CASE CLOSED

I opened the door, cautiously, smelling the copper-penny odor of new violence. My breath came in quick gulps. I took my gun from my shoulder bag. A few years of experience on the L.A.P.D. and a gun in one's hand have a way of conferring confidence, if not a feeling of invincibility. So I slipped in fast, around the door frame, gun leveled.

Sandy Renkowski lay facedown on the floor, the back of her pink blouse sliced and bloody with multiple stab wounds, that verdict easily come by because a blood-smeared butcher knife lay on the beige carpet next to her body, along with pieces of a ceramic lamp base.

Part of the base was intact, the bulb still lit, shining upward like a spotlight on the woman who sat on the couch—Bobbi Calder, blinking at me, her face all sharp, bony shadows in the eerie glow.

★

MAXINE O'CALLAGHAN
SET-UP

WORLDWIDE ®

TORONTO • NEW YORK • LONDON
AMSTERDAM • PARIS • SYDNEY • HAMBURG
STOCKHOLM • ATHENS • TOKYO • MILAN
MADRID • WARSAW • BUDAPEST • AUCKLAND

SET-UP

A Worldwide Mystery/May 1994

First published by St. Martin's Press, Incorporated.

ISBN 0-373-26144-6

Printed in U.S.A.

For my friends Judy Schneyer and
Mollie Aghadjian, who provide good advice and
loyal support and are always willing to share steamed
veggies and chocolate eclairs at lunch.

Special thanks to Bruce Haskett, talented writer and
real-life P.I. who willingly shares his expertise and
resources. Any mistakes in weaving that advice into
my story are, of course, my own.

ONE

I SAT in my new Astro van on the street outside County Supervisor Sam Newley's office, waiting for Sandy Renkowski to make her daily messenger run to the Civic Center, not looking forward to what I was about to do. Well, it was my job. I didn't have to like it.

After two weeks undercover as a temp clerk in Newley's office, I'd have preferred nailing several people other than Sandy on his staff. Newley's assistant, Tony Vero, topped the list. Too bad Vero was the one who suggested calling in a P.I. to investigate the shortages in the cash contributions for the Save Our Parks Fund, Newley's pet project.

To make matters worse, not only was Sandy late, I had a much more immediate problem. I squirmed, sighed, adjusted the visor against the glare that wasn't completely blocked by the leafy shade of an old pepper tree, mopped the sweat trickling down from my hairline just in front of my ears, and wondered how much longer I could hold out before finding a bathroom.

A man can bring along an old mason jar. Jack used to, back when stakeouts were a team effort, back when I was the female half of West and West Detective Agency. Six years now. A long time ago.

Of course, on a real surveillance the rule is to forgo food and drink to avoid this kind of problem. But I hadn't planned on waiting for two hours. And, in addition, I'd made the mistake of stopping for breakfast earlier at Mom's Kounty Kooking. A little over a year ago I'd eked out a living with a side job there, and I still like to drop in and see my old friends. Happy to see me too, they keep the coffee coming. Thanks, guys.

Just when I was gloomily contemplating making a Port-a-Potty a standard addition to my stakeout survival kit, the car phone rang.

"She's coming out," Vero said. "And, remember, Mr. Newley wants this handled as quietly as possible."

"I'll do my best. How about the police?"

"On their way."

"Any news on the subpoena?"

"It's ready to be served."

I was sure the subpoena being served on Sandy's bank would show recent deposits to her savings account because I'd already had a check done via computer. I don't like electronic snooping, and, frankly, I distrust the easy slyness of hacking. It's also illegal, but then so are a lot of other things in the P.I. trade.

I got out of the van, slung my purse over my shoulder, and trudged across the street.

No shade over there. The hot June sun burned down, and a strong tarry scent drifted up from the softening asphalt. Even in my Banana Republic open-weave cotton slacks and sleeveless shirt, I felt the brand of the heat against my skin. My thirty-eight added a comforting weight to the purse. I certainly didn't expect to have to use a gun, but I'd made a few too many mistakes in judgment recently, so I needed the reassurance.

Sandy came out the front of the building and headed my way, squinting against the glare, putting on her sunglasses. She was petite and graceful, dressed in a melon-colored skirt and short-sleeved cropped jacket, her honey blond hair pulled up off her face with a banana clip. She moved over to let me pass, not recognizing me until I said, "Sandy," and stopped directly in front of her.

"Delilah? Sorry, I didn't see you there. I thought your assignment was over. Are you coming back to work?"

"Not exactly." I hesitated, but there was no easy way to say it. "Sandy, the police will be here in a minute. Until they arrive, I want you to stay right here with me."

She stared at me. *"What?"*

"Would you give me your handbag, please?" A precaution just in case she decided to throw it into a passing pickup, but no legal way I could insist if she refused.

"My bag? Police?" She sounded bewildered, but she did what I asked. "I don't understand—" It was coming to her, however, because after a moment she said, "But why? All I did was—"

She broke off because a squad car came barreling up, no sirens but moving very fast and sliding expertly into the curb. Two Garden Grove patrolmen made the actual arrest, checking her handbag for the marked money we had planted in the incoming contributions, reading her her rights.

Sandy's bewilderment gave way to rising panic. "This is *crazy*. I'm not a thief. Delilah—"

"Watch your head," one of the patrolman cautioned as they quickly and efficiently bundled her into the car. The last I saw of her was her stunned face turned abstract by the fierce glare on the car window.

By rights I should have gone on up and given my report to Sam Newley in person. But, client or not, and despite the fact that he had racked up a lot of great PR recently with his campaign to raise money to rejuvenate Orange County's budget-starved park system, I really didn't care for the man any more than I liked his assistant. And, besides, I had a more urgent problem. So I gave Tony Vero a terse accounting over the car phone on my way to a pit stop at the nearest McDonald's.

ONE WEEK and one well-heeled client later I decided I deserved a day off, so when Rita called and asked me to drive down to Laguna for lunch, I accepted. In honor of the occasion, I even abandoned my standard casual wear of blue jeans, tank top, and running shoes for a sundress and sandals.

Since this smacked of dressing up, I also felt obliged to add some blush, eyeshadow, and liner for my beer-bottle brown eyes. As for my hair, I'm wearing it wash and wear, short and punky on top, then layered to brush back at the sides. At thirty-six I'm already plucking an occasional white strand from the cinnamon brown. Depressing.

I went out to wait for Rita, just locking the door when she drove up in her new red Miata, right on time as usual.

Besides being a long-time friend, Rita Braddock runs the answering service I use for my office. In an age where even ten-year-olds have their own answering machine, she has found a select group of customers who still prefer to have their calls answered by a human voice and are willing to pay for the extra amenity—like me, although for old times' sake I get a discount.

Getting into her car, I said, "Nice."

She gave me a wry grin and gestured out the window at the condo complex where I live. "A long way for both of us, Delilah."

I nodded agreement. Our lives had changed radically, especially mine, so I could casually use all those magic words: Astro van, condo, car phone. Eighteen months ago I could barely put gas in my old

Mustang. In addition to moonlighting as a waitress, I had been camping out in my office and bumming bathroom privileges from my friends. Now I've hired an assistant, half-time while he finishes up his degree at UC Irvine with a double major in business and computer science. And I can afford to take a day off if I want to.

Rita's life had turned around three years ago when she met Farley Truitt, who was ten years younger. After she started sharing Farley's tofu and bean sprouts and his passion for aerobics, she dropped twenty-five pounds and looked Farley's age. Then about eight months ago she let him talk her into putting up the money for their own health spa, which I thought was financial suicide but turned out to be a first-class ticket to the good life in Orange County.

As for my own change of fortune, I keep telling myself it's because I'm good at what I do, and the word has finally gotten around. That works for a few insurance clients and worried women checking out a lover's financial background, but then, of course, there are people like Sam Newley. The big ones with money.

Rita and I made small talk as she maneuvered through the traffic—the health spa, my latest cases—although I avoided the subject of Sandy Renkowski, and she tactfully didn't mention my off-and-on relationship with Matthew Scott. Rita looked great in linen oatmeal slacks and a tropical print blouse. Her hair was longer and several shades lighter, the kind of cut and curl that only money can buy.

She seemed a little tense, which was easily explained by the fact that it's always rush hour in Orange County these days, with clogged freeways and gridlocked streets. Or maybe she was nervous because of her spiffy new car. By the time we made Coast Highway and headed south, I thought it must be more than that. She'd stopped chatting and gripped the steering wheel, her gaze fixed intently on the view out the windshield, although I suspected she was thinking about something else, rather than enjoying the sweep of ocean bordering a rare piece of undeveloped land north of Laguna.

We made a fine pair, because I was having a sobering moment of my own as we passed a narrow asphalt road that angled off through the sun-burnt brush and wound up the coastal hills. I knew that, farther up, there was a guard gate, and I also knew just where to look to get a glimpse of the huge house with its ten million dollar view.

Erik Lundstrom lived up there, the man who had appointed himself my fairy godfather and was quietly making sure my name was mentioned in all the right places. I met Erik through my old pal, Charlie Colfax, as in the Colfax Agency, as in the largest private investigation firm in Orange County. Charlie was doing a favor for me, or so he said. Seems Erik had a security opening. Erik and I got along famously, and he offered me the job.

Giving up my agency was a necessary albeit painful decision. I planned to do it, to totally rearrange my life, and while some of this was economic necessity, I was also more than a little attracted to the wealthy, powerful, absolutely gorgeous Mr. Lundstrom and had reason to believe the feeling was mutual.

Then I discovered the job offer had been cooked up by Charlie and Erik to distract me from the case I was working on, and that Erik was involved with somebody else all the time he was batting those beautiful baby blues at me. I cut my connections with Erik quickly and cleanly. Or so I thought at the time.

I'm not sure if Erik helps me out of guilt or if he just can't bear to have a budding relationship end except on his own terms. Maybe he even has some romanticized notion of what might have been. I'm not sure I care. Because, in spite of Erik's behind-the-scenes assistance, I work hard and give a good return for my clients' money.

Like the job this week. And the one for Supervisor Newley. And never mind Sandy Renkowski's abject face through that patrol car window.

Well, forget Sandy. And Erik. And Matt, come to think of it, because even though we were "on" at the moment, I had the feeling we were fast sliding toward "off" again. This was my free day, and I was determined to enjoy the brilliant sunshine, an ocean full of jade green waves crested with frothy white, and air that blew across a thousand miles of water and smelled only of sea salt. After a bottle of wine and some fresh swordfish, I'd bet both Rita and I would feel a hell of a lot better.

Wrong again.

Rita waited until we turned off Coast Highway, heading for the Beach House's valet parking to say, "I'm sorry, Delilah. I'm afraid this isn't just lunch for the two of us."

I groaned. "Please don't tell me I have to eat rubber chicken and listen to somebody talk about saving the whales."

Another side to Rita's relationship with Farley included Greenpeace bumper stickers and fund-raisers for every endangered species known to man.

"Nothing like that," she said.

The valet stood, holding her door open, waiting expectantly. This being Laguna Beach, he wore shorts and a T-shirt, and his teeth shone whitely against his surfer tan as he cast an admiring eye over the car.

We got out and stood there while he took the Miata off to parts unknown.

"Are you going to tell me?" I asked. "Or do I have to guess?"

"Somebody's joining us. Her name is Bobbi Calder." She looked at me expectantly.

The name pinged dimly, but I didn't know why. I shook my head.

"Operation Slo-Grow," Rita added, and then I had it.

Besides being on the city council in Laguna, Bobbi—short for Roberta—Calder headed up a countywide organization to slow the development that was gobbling up the open spaces and strawberry farms.

"And?" I prodded.

"She's got some problems, and I think you're the one to help her."

"That's flattering," I said. "But I have a perfectly good office she can visit, complete with an assistant and a computer. I even have a new Mr. Coffee."

"I had a hard enough time getting her to meet you over lunch. The woman is even more stubborn than you are, Delilah, and that's saying a lot. Will you talk to her?"

The valet was back, giving us a curious look. The buildings walled off the ocean breeze and trapped the heat, so I said, "Fine. I'll be happy to. Just as long as I can do it over something cold with plenty of ice."

Eyeing the waiting people who spilled out into a grotto full of brilliant bougainvillea, I figured an hour's holding pattern, but Bobbi had already staked out a corner table next to the patio. The whole dining area was open-air, covered with canvas to cut the glare. Space heaters provided warmth on cold evenings and sliding doors gave protection from chilly ocean breezes. I don't know what happens when it rains. Today all the doors were wide open.

Bobbi stood up as we approached. She was tall, with the rawboned leanness of a woman who would have plowed fields and raised a dozen children a century ago, and she wore a denim skirt and a white shirt that made me feel frivolous and overdressed. Dark hair streaked with gray was swept up in a knot on top of her head. She wore no makeup, not even lipstick, and looked at you straight on with dark, intelligent eyes. I expect she didn't give a damn about the crinkles at the corners of her eyes or the fine cross hatching in her tanned skin. Her only jewelry was a pair of dangling Najavo earrings of turquoise and silver.

I was remembering some of her recent press now. During the latest attempt to carve up Laguna Canyon, she'd led a protest and lain down in front of the bulldozers, yielding a photo that ran in all the papers.

She waited until we were settled with menus, ice water, glasses of Chardonnay, and a basket of sourdough bread before she said, "I'm going to be straight with you, Ms. West. I'm only here because Rita kept bugging me about meeting you. In the first place I'm not sure I need a private detective."

Ms. West. Nice and polite. Also cool, distant.

"You need somebody," Rita put in.

"Maybe. Even so, I don't think Ms. West is that person."

The way she said it got my hackles up, or maybe it was something in that level gaze that classified me as some kind of creepy-crawly that she'd like to swat with a handy newspaper.

"You may be right. But I'm curious how you came to that decision after—" I checked my watch—"after knowing me about five minutes."

"I asked around," Bobbi said. "Frankly, I don't care much for the kind of people you work for."

Aha! I was beginning to get the drift. Remembering her press, I also remembered the ongoing feud with the County Board of Supervisors. "People like Sam Newley, for instance?"

"For one," she said shortly.

"He's a client,' I said. "That doesn't mean we're buddies."

"And your job for him? Nothing about that bothered you?"

I wasn't surprised that she knew about the incident involving Sandy. It was a matter of public record. To tell the truth, what really surprised me was that the press hadn't latched on to it yet.

"I caught a thief," I said, more angry than I had a right to be. "The woman was stealing money contributed by senior citizens and school children. But if you have a problem with my part in having her arrested, by all means find somebody else."

"Okay, enough." Rita glared at us. "I was right. The two of you are perfect for each other, a couple of stubborn mules. Bobbi, will you at least talk to Delilah about what's going on? And cut out the Ms. West shit."

A pause, then Bobbi admitted, "Somebody's threatening me."

"What kind of threats?"

When Bobbi hesitated again, Rita said, "A letter bomb. It came to her office."

"More like a letter fizzle," Bobbi said dryly. "It was just a hoax. I don't know why Rita's so worried about it."

"Maybe you ought to worry," I said. "Did you report this to the police?"

"I thought about it. To tell the truth, it was the publicity I thought about. Anything to generate sympathy for Slo-Grow. But I decided against it. Too many kooks out there. No sense giving them ideas."

"What if it was a warning? Maybe the next one will be for real."

A bold gull hopped in from the patio and regarded us with shiny black eyes. Bobbi took some bread from the basket, tore off a crust, and tossed it to him.

"I'm an old hand at protests." She watched the gull as it took the morsel, made a quick exit, and flapped off. "Civil rights, Viet Nam. I've been kicked, beaten, teargassed, arrested. You have to decide early on if what you believe in is worth the price."

"Are the stakes really that high this time? You could be right, and this could be a hoax, but is it worth risking your life?"

She picked up the menu, opened it, and looked at me over the top. Something had changed in her estimation of me. She wasn't ready to declare us blood sisters, but she was, at least, reserving judgment.

"After lunch," she said, "I'll take you for a drive."

TWO

BOBBI HAD an old Toyota Landcruiser with a soft top snapped on and the sides left open. She climbed up with practiced ease, but Rita and I had to clamber aboard. At least Rita'd had the good sense to wear slacks.

I sat on the hard front seat next to Bobbi; Rita perched in back. No automatic transmission on this baby, but Bobbi shifted gears smoothly as we cut through Laguna on side streets and headed inland, out of town. The noise of the engine and rushing air combined to preclude much conversation.

Leaving Laguna, the canyon road curved past a body repair shop, a nursery, an animal shelter. Houses clung to the sides of the hills, a few new ones among the old and ramshackle. On the left past the angular buildings of the Art Institute, the canyon reverted to its natural state: enormous sandstone boulders and outcroppings, big old live oaks, a tangle of vines and thistles growing over a line of fencing, a few cows browsing on the tall, yellowing grass. I've been told that early in the morning you can still see deer grazing among the cattle.

Once through the narrow width of the coastal range, we swung right and almost immediately could

see the housing tracts, row upon row, a red-tiled river
flowing toward the sea. Bobbi turned again, roughly
paralleling the ocean on the other side of the range,
driving on brand new six-lane roads, harbingers of
the traffic that was to come. Up on the inland flanks
of the hills, huge caterpillars were peeling away
grasses and chaparral and rearranging the sprawling
masses into orderly tiers. Some sections, almost
ready for the wood and cement, revealed the skele-
tal white clay beneath the outer skin of vegetation,
like some huge animal stripped down to the bone.

Bobbi stopped the jeep and sat, staring up at a
partially denuded hillside where at least fifteen machines, looking like huge, prehistoric insects, chewed
away.

"A tribe in the Amazon has a name for the white
man," Bobbi said. "They call us the termite people." A brief silence, then: "The average cost of a
house in Orange County is two-hundred-fifty thousand and climbing. The *average*. Count the lots up
there and start multiplying."

"I don't think I can count that high," Rita said.

Bobbi shifted into first gear and drove away, her
face grim. "They'll never stop until every square foot
is paved over and sold."

I didn't answer. This was Bobbi's show. Anyway,
I knew she was right, although I wasn't sure there
was a damn thing anybody could do about it.

We retraced our route back into the canyon. She
stopped again alongside the road. Looking back into

an unspoiled pocket of meadow with a redtailed hawk circling lazily above, you could almost forget the roar of cars whizzing past on the other side of the jeep.

"Take a good look," Bobbi said. "There are still a few thousand acres left. Here and over by the Santa Anas. If I can do anything to save those acres, I damn well will."

"Then you'd better stay in one piece," I said. "Rita's right. You need some help."

It occurred to me then just how many hours might be involved in this kind of investigation. I had a feeling Roberta Calder wasn't rich, and I knew her Slo-Grow organization certainly wasn't supported by the county fat cats. My work was bringing in considerably more money these days than Bobbi could afford. Also, I have landlords, loan companies, and a very nice computer science/business major to support.

It also occurred to me in another sickening flash that I was suckling on the hind teat of the county's big fat economic hog just like everybody else, and it was development dollars that fattened the beast.

"I'd like to help you," I said. "If you want me to."

"I'll have to think about it and talk to some of my people." That measuring glance again. "I'll let you know."

ON THE DRIVE DOWN to Laguna I'd been busy enjoying the sunshine and the view of the ocean. On the way back I sat on the side of the car facing inland. Just north of Laguna I caught sight of another swarm of caterpillars working, and saw red stakes marking out another hillside soon to go under the blade. No inexpensive little two-hundred-fifty-thousand-dollar crackerboxes here. Try a million, plus. At least a good-sized portion of the coastline had been preserved for a county park. That was something, anyway.

And then there was Erik Lundstrom's land, a big enough chunk of acreage so he'd never have to worry about the bulldozers moving in or tracts spoiling his view. He'd see the houses at a distance, the night lights like a wash of diamonds against the dark sea, only worth a whole lot more.

I didn't know for certain that Erik was in on the coast development, or the ones we'd looked at that afternoon. But there was damned little in Orange County that he didn't have a hand in.

Hell.

"What are you looking so glum about?" Rita asked. "I thought it went pretty well, considering."

"Something about me sticks in her throat." I stared off up into the hills. "And I don't think it's just that I worked for Sam Newley. Do you know what it is?"

"No. Afraid not."

Just for an instant the sun struck sparks from the windows of the house up there.

"You ever hear from him?" Rita asked.

I looked back at the road. My cheeks burned a little, but I hoped I had gotten enough sun that day so she wouldn't notice.

"No."

"Would you like to?"

"I'd like to change the subject," I said firmly.

She gave me her sidelong, you-can't-fool-me glance while I switched the conversation to traffic, her car, the health spa. We hadn't spent much time together lately, so there was lots to catch up on.

I didn't notice until later, after she dropped me off at the condo, that once again we hadn't talked about Matt. More telling was the fact that I hadn't thought about him either until I went into my living room, kicked off my shoes, and, barefoot, stepped on a half-chewed piece of rawhide chip left by Matt's little dog the last time the two of them had spent the night.

I definitely did not want to pursue that line of thought. Rubbing my foot, I hopped over to the couch, reached for the portable phone that sat on an end table, and dialed the office. Danny Thu answered on the second ring. He said things had been very quiet. He had been working away on a program that would enable us to tap into all kinds of county, state, and federal information networks. I assumed this was all on the up-and-up. If it wasn't, I didn't want to know.

Danny was twenty. He had been born in Saigon, but his parents had been fortunate enough to make it out on one of the last planes before the Cong swept in. Lucky Danny. Lucky me that he had answered my ad. With his smarts, he could have had a job anywhere. I still haven't figured out why he took one with me. Maybe, growing up, he watched too many episodes of "The Rockford Files" and "Magnum, P.I."

"Messages," Danny said. Two more prospective clients, big corporate accounts that I'd probably lose if I got hung up on the Calder case, one from Sam Newley's accountant questioning some of my expenses, and "—this is kinda weird," Danny went on, "Sandy Renkowski called. I tried to find out why, but she wouldn't tell me anything. You want the number?"

"I guess so."

I wrote it down, said good-bye to Danny, and sat there with the phone in my hand, debating. I knew Sandy had made bail. Why was she calling me? Maybe just to protest her innocence. In any case I might as well let her know, politely but firmly, that I had no intention of discussing the case with her.

I dialed and got a busy signal. Later, then. I wasn't going to waste my day off waiting for Sandy to stop gabbing and hang up.

I spent the rest of the afternoon swimming laps in the complex's pool and getting some rays, properly sunscreened, of course. After a shower, I drank some orange juice and thought about dinner. Danny's brother owns a restaurant in Little Saigon. Or, if I called Jorge, my friend who runs the kitchen at Mom's, I'd be sure to get an invitation to come over to his house for dinner with him and Consuelo and the kids. I could even cook. I do a pretty mean scrambled egg when I put my mind to it.

While I decided, I checked with Rita's service. Nothing urgent. And nothing from Bobbi Calder. Or Matt. Or Sandy Renkowski. I picked up the note-pad that contained her number and tried it again. Busy. Well, to hell with it.

I needed laughter, I decided. Friends. A bottle of Corona beer wouldn't be bad either. I called Jorge, who said he was just baking the tortillas and with the traffic the way it was I'd better get going.

DINNER WAS SERVED with a happy babble of bilin-gual conversation. Consuelo doesn't speak much English, so the kids translate. Everybody wanted to tell me what was happening in school and at work, and the kids always want to hear about my cases. They catch old Jimmy Rockford and Tommy Mag-num on reruns.

"We take a vacation next month," Jorge said.

"Vacation." Consuelo picked up the word, nod-ding, smiling happily. "En Mexicali."

"We're going to see my grandma," the youngest, Isabel, put in. "And all my aunts and uncles too."

The trip was another sign of prosperity for them, along with the new sofa and TV in the living room and Isabel's first bicycle, a shiny Schwinn.

"Hey, what about I call everybody for a game?" Jorge said. "Just like old times."

A poker game with the kitchen help at Mom's once the cafe closed used to keep me in eating money.

"It would be fun," I said, "but I think I'll let you guys off the hook."

Jorge laughed. "Better times for all of us, mi amiga. We'll do it soon—for the fun of it, okay?"

I promised we would and got up to help clear the table.

After the dishes were done and the kids chased off to do their homework, I agreed to a final cup of coffee and asked to use the phone while it brewed. The busy signal from Sandy Renkowski's phone didn't raise any alarms. No reason why it should. Mostly the sound irritated me. She'd been so anxious to get in touch with me, and now I thought she'd probably left her receiver off the hook. The operator verified my suspicion.

Jorge announced the coffee was ready. He looked tired, having gotten up at four-thirty that morning. So did Consuelo. A long day for both of them, so I said good-bye and left. It was still early, only a little before eight, and, as I drove away, the sun, hanging somewhere out over the Pacific, filled the tree-lined streets with touches of gold amid the long shadows. Then I rounded a corner and got a view of the Santa Ana Mountains. Looking through that accumulated golden haze, I could see it for what it was: an ugly brown layer of smog.

I thought about Jorge and Consuelo. The Sanchezes were getting their share of the Orange County boom, too, with more people crowding the restaurants, more big new houses needing the cleaning service that hired Consuelo. If Bobbi Calder's Slo-Grow organization had its way, the Sanchezes might be breathing better but eating less, and there would certainly be no new bikes for the kids.

Determined not to let my mind get stuck in that groove, I headed in the general direction of the nearest mall, considering a movie. A few more blocks and I remembered that Sandy's apartment building was really on the way.

I'd done backgrounds on the people in Newley's office before narrowing the investigation down to Sandy, so I knew where she lived. I'd talked to a few of her neighbors, most of whom had only the vaguest idea who she was, one guy remembering her only as that foxy little blond in 24D. I knew the kind of car she drove, that she had a cat even though pets were forbidden, that she was quiet and had no loud parties or frequent sleepovers by either male or female guests. The subpoenaed bank records had verified that Sandy had been making regular deposits to her savings account, amounts that added up to a lot more than her income, and the marked money in her purse when she was arrested confirmed where the deposits were coming from.

Stupid to go by and see the woman, of course. If she hadn't left her phone off the hook deliberately, she'd bumped it, or the cat had. I could call her to-morrow. Even better, I could wait for her to call me back, and hope she never would.

Still...

Yeah, still, and don't ask me to explain it, I wanted to talk to Sandy. Something she'd said that last day, or the way she'd looked at me, some vague uneasi-ness that had crept into my mind and stuck like one of those burrs that Matt's little dog gets in his fur and has to have cut out.

Streetlights were coming on as I left my van on the street and walked along the edge of the Garden View Apartments' parking lot. The building was a wood and stucco U, two floors, with a swimming pool in the middle, reminiscent of a sixties motel. I didn't see anything resembling a garden unless you counted an occasional bird of paradise and two Mexican fan palms next to the pool.

Marked stalls on all three outer sides of the park-ing lot were full of cars at this time of the day. In a shadowy streetside corner, the stall labeled 24D held Sandy's little blue Ford Escort. Beside it, a stumpy eucalyptus shed long, red-veined leaves and papery bark and exuded a smell like moldy wood smeared with Noxzema.

A pool party was in progress. As I climbed up a wide wooden staircase to the second floor, I could hear laughter and the *whomp* of water as somebody jumped in. The apartments were placed back to back, one set facing the pool, one with a view of the parking area. Sandy was in back where the party noise was muffled.

Twilight was going fast. A covered walkway served the apartments, lit by low-wattage bulbs and a wash of yellow illumination from the sodium vapor lamps in the parking lot. A light burned behind Sandy's tightly closed blinds. I knocked, waited, heard nothing except the plaintive meowing of a cat on the other side of the door.

Maybe Sandy was down at the party, having a good time. Or off seeing the movie I was missing. I knocked again in case she was in the bedroom or the shower. The cat's meow changed to a wail that sent a primal crawl of dread snaking up my neck.

I thought about going for the manager, or calling the police, or risking a breaking-and-entering charge, all of that put on hold while I tried the obvious and reached for the door knob.

It turned. I opened the door, cautiously, smelling the copper penny odor of new violence, glimpsing the room bathed with surrealistic light as the cat shot past me. I quickly stepped back, up against the wall next to the door frame. My breath came in quick gulps. I took my gun from my shoulder bag.

A reasonable person would head back to the car phone in the van, call the cops, and stay safely away until they arrived. I heard a siren in the distance, however, so maybe the patrol car assigned to this area would be busy with something that had higher priority. Anyway, a few years of experience on the L.A.P.D. and a gun in one's hand have a way of conferring confidence, if not a feeling of invincibility. So I slipped in fast, around the door frame, gun leveled.

Sandy Renkowski lay face down on the floor, the back of her pink blouse sliced and bloody with multiple stab wounds, that verdict easily come by because a blood-smeared butcher knife lay on the beige carpet next to her body, along with pieces of a ceramic lamp base.

Part of the base was intact, the bulb still lit, shining upward from the floor through the askew shade like a spotlight on the woman who sat on the couch—Bobbi Calder, blinking at me, her face all sharp, bony shadows in the eerie glow.

THREE

"BOBBI?"

She stared at me, owl-like. The stark light hollowed her cheeks and accentuated the wrinkles that radiated from the corners of her eyes, a preview of what she would look like twenty-five years from now.

I did a quick sweep of the place: kitchen, bedroom, bath. Nobody there but the three of us—make that two, because Sandy was dead. I knelt to check for a pulse anyway, found nothing. Her head was turned to one side, the one visible eye fixed and staring behind a veil of fine, blond hair.

All this time the siren got louder, very close now, Jesus, right in the parking lot outside, and then it died in mid-yowl. Through the open door behind me I caught the flash of strobing lights.

"Bobbi, snap out of it," I said urgently.

She didn't respond. She just sat, twisting her hands together, and I saw the smudges she'd left on her jeans skirt, dark purple against the denim blue.

"My God—Bobbi, did you touch the knife?"

"I thought—I wanted to—to help her." Her voice sounded rusty, unused. "I had to do something."

"Jesus, you did."

She'd pulled the knife from Sandy's back. The
question was, of course, had she put it there in the
first place? If she hadn't, so what? She wasn't exactly my client, not my problem. Still—*wipe the
damn thing clean*—tampering with evidence, won-
derful. I might've done it anyway. I might even have
put my thirty-eight away, a better idea, but heavy
footsteps thumped on the wooden balcony, coming
fast, and then a male voice bellowed, "Police!
Freeze!"

His forty-five looked like the business end of a
cannon so I did exactly what he said: put my gun on
the floor nice and easy, kicked it over to him, lay face
down, obligingly put my hands behind my head. I
told him quietly that I was a private detective, that I
had a permit for the gun, that my identification was
in my purse.

None of this cut any ice at all. He manacled my
wrists with a large plastic zip tie, ordered me to stay
where I was, muttered, "Christ," as he glanced down
at Sandy.

"It's all my fault," Bobbi said.

This woman was willing to put her life on the line
for other people's civil rights, for the preservation of
wild canyons that provided homes for deer and coyotes and birds. Was that just a great facade hiding
some secret core so dark she could stab Sandy to
death?

I had to admit the possibility; still, I said, "Bobbi,
don't say anything else."

"But I'm responsible," she insisted.

This got her zip-tied too, while I told the cop, "She's in shock. She doesn't know what she's saying."

"Yeah? Well, you're the one better keep their mouth shut while we sort this out."

He got on his radio to call for detectives, forensics, and backup. I figured he was fresh out of the academy, first year on patrol, a kid with a big sweat stain on the back of his sharply pressed khakis, his skin a little chalky against his dark hair and moustache.

"She was so scared. I know she blamed me." Bobbi rocked back and forth, talking to herself. "I kept telling her we'd get the best attorney, but she wouldn't listen. Why wouldn't she listen to me?"

"Bobbi, shut *up*," I said.

I heard more sirens and the squeal of tires outside. Lots of footsteps and the excited buzz of massing spectators. The young cop stomped around nervously. About a half-dozen uniforms arrived. A couple of them herded people back. The rest jammed inside the small living room, made even more crowded by the tipped-over furniture. One bumped the lamp that lay on the floor, sending the light tilting crazily.

I thought it might occur to one of them sooner or later that Sandy had been stabbed, not shot. It didn't, and any protest from me only brought threats and reprimands. My shoulders ached from being wrenched behind my back, and I sincerely regretted that second helping of carne asada because Sandy's corpse lay just two feet away, the brassy scent of her blood strong in my nose.

At least Bobbi had retreated back toward catatonia and was keeping her mouth closed. I couldn't see her face any longer, just her feet pressed so tightly together her ankle bones looked white.

Then I heard a familiar voice ordering the unnecessary cops out of the room, recognizing it before I saw Lieutenant Brady's scuffed Florsheims among the spit-shined, patrol officer issues. After the young cop gave him all the details of how he'd captured the two lady desperados single-handedly, Brady hunkered down beside me, a bulky man in a limp gray suit, his bald head shiny in the unshaded light. "Well, Mrs. West, having a nice little rest?"

"Oh, yeah, great. Now are you going to let me up, or do I start thinking lawsuit?"

"What do you expect? At the scene of a crime, waving a gun around." At least he restrained himself from the tsk-tsk's as he undid the ties and gave me a hand up. "Your permit *is* up to date?"

I rubbed my wrists. "You ought to know."

I'd had a lot of trouble earlier that year at renewal time, and I was pretty sure Brady was responsible.

"Oh, yeah, that's right." He'd shaved off his walrus moustache, so I got the full effect of his snide smile. "You've got a power player greasing the wheels, don't you?"

Gun permits in Orange County are getting scarce. One local P.I. had sued recently over his denial and won the suit by pointing out that a good many of the available permits were going to the sheriff's friends and political cronies. Yet my application had gone through despite Brady's roadblocks. Erik Lundstrom again? I wouldn't take bets.

"How I got the permit isn't the issue," I said. "I have it. And since it's obvious my gun isn't the murder weapon, I want it back."

"In time. And nothing's for sure until I hear it from the medical examiner. Now suppose you tell me what you're doing here."

"Roberta Calder's my client." I hadn't time to tamper with the evidence. Might as well have a go at perjury. "You ought to know she's on the city council in Laguna Beach."

"Oh, *that* Roberta Calder."

"Delilah?" The sound of her name roused Bobbi a little.

"You just sit there and take it easy," I told her. "I'll handle this now." To Brady: "She phoned me to say she'd discovered Sandy's body."

Jesus.

We are not talking professional behavior here. My lie was a great intuitive leap that could easily turn into the world's biggest pratfall.

"Sandy—that's the victim?" he asked.

I nodded. "Sandy Renkowski. I advised Miss Calder to call the police, which I presume she did since you're here—"

I left it hanging, hoping he might throw me a crumb of information. Well, *somebody* had called them. Maybe it had been Bobbi. All I got from Brady was an enigmatic smile.

"—then I came right over," I finished.

"And found it necessary to pull a gun on your client when you arrived."

"Just a precaution. She was incoherent over the phone. I didn't know what I was getting into."

"Un-huh." The weary cynicism in his eyes said he wasn't buying it. He glanced over at Bobbi, who still looked confused and disoriented. The young patrolman hovered near the couch with his hand on his gun butt as though he expected her to jump up any time now and make her escape through the cordon of police who blocked the door.

"You can see she's in a state of shock," I said.

"According to Officer Meacham—" he indicated the young cop—"Miss Calder was rational enough to make some pretty damaging statements."

"She said she did it, lieutenant," Meacham put in. "From the looks of her hands, she did too."

This was a reasonable assumption. So much so that I had to wonder why I was committing a felony by covering for the woman. Damned if I knew.

"Forget what she said," I told Brady. "Meacham didn't Mirandize her, so you'll never use her statement in court."

"But I didn't arrest her," Meacham said. "I got to arrest her first." He shot Brady a flustered, fearful look.

"Which might've been a good idea," Brady said sourly.

"I hope you plan to have her attorney here before you ask any more questions," I said.

"Yeah, right. We'll do it by the book. But if we find her prints on the knife—"

"Oh, you'll find them," I said. "She thought Sandy was alive, and she had some idea that pulling out the knife would help her."

"Wasn't that thoughtful?" He broke off as the forensic crew arrived, nodding his hellos to them. "Getting a little crowded, so what say we continue this down at the station, Mrs. West?"

"Are we under arrest?"

"Your client, definitely. You—have it any way you like. You want your rights and your attorney, too? Or maybe you'd like to call up your godfather—the one who's so good with gun permits."

I felt color rise in my cheeks. "I'll just wing it, Brady. I'm always happy to cooperate with the police."

He made a formal little show of charging Bobbi and reading her rights, the ritual familiarized by every cop show on TV. Bobbi recognized the words all right. For the first time, panic replaced confusion as Brady helped her up and steered her toward the door.

"Delilah," she said, "my God, what's happening?"

"It's a mistake. Don't worry. We'll get it straightened out." I followed close behind.

"But Sandy—" She pulled against Brady's grasp, looking back. "*Ohmygod San*-DEE—" The last word growing to a wail.

"Come on." I grabbed her other arm and helped Brady hustle her out.

The full horror of Sandy's brutal murder had finally penetrated her fugue. By the time we pushed through the cops and spectators and got to the stairs, her breath came in ragged gasps, and tears rained down her face. By the time we reached the patrol car, she was sobbing. Either she was doing Academy Award-caliber acting or the great heaving sobs were ones of grief and loss.

Even Brady wasn't a big enough shit to make her ride alone. So I sat with her in the back of the black and white, put my arms around her, and held her while she cried.

FOUR

TELLING LIES is a lot like eating potato chips. One never quite does the trick. Since I'd told Brady that Bobbi called me to report finding Sandy's body, naturally I had to tell him where I'd received the call. What he demanded was a minute-by-minute accounting of my movements since I got out of bed that morning, and I listed everything accurately until I got to Bobbi's call.

I could fudge the time I left the Sanchezes a little but not enough to say I'd driven back to my office. I had to tell him I'd gone home.

His bushy eyebrows rose. "She only became your client this afternoon, and already she has your home telephone number?"

I shrugged. "Service is my business."

"Right. Tell me again about going to Miss Renkowski's apartment."

I did, for the fourth or fifth time. I'd lost count.

I shifted on the hard-backed, thin-cushioned chair and massaged my left temple with my fingertips, thinking that this was maybe not the stupidest thing I'd ever done, but it came close.

My head ached from the harsh fluorescent overhead lights and the stale cigarette smoke that lingered in the empty squad room. No, I didn't know Bobbi's relationship with Sandy; she hadn't mentioned Sandy at lunch, and she was too hysterical to be questioned about it at the scene.

Of course, I was leaving out my own connection with Sandy. He'd find out about it soon enough. If I told him now, I'd be in for an all-nighter, trying to satisfy his cop's natural suspicion of coincidence. Besides, I like to know some of the answers myself before I have to field questions from the police.

One thing had come clear to me: the reason for Bobbi's hostility earlier. She'd known firsthand about my part in getting Sandy busted.

I glanced at my watch. Ten past midnight. Brady had turned Bobbi over to be processed, making sure her attorney was called and asking to be notified when he showed up. Since then he had devoted his attention to me, steadily refusing to let me see Bobbi. A good way for him to kill time, I guess, and where the hell was Bobbi's lawyer?

Across his desk, Brady stared at me with hooded eyes. He looked tired too, his skin a little gray and jowly, but he said doggedly, "Okay, one more time."

His intercom buzzed, saving me from another recital. Bobbi's attorney had finally arrived.

Harvey Klein came into the squad room, a short, wiry man dressed in a beautiful dark blue pinstripe suit, snowy shirt, and a silk burgundy tie. He looked haggard, his tanned skin ashy with shock.

"I was in L.A. at the Music Centre," he explained. "Left my beeper, so I didn't know about this until I got home. I'd like to know the charges against my client."

Brady handed him the official report. Klein read it, glancing up at me. The pain in those expressive brown eyes told me he was more than Bobbi's attorney.

"You're Delilah West?" he asked.

"Yes. We need to talk before you see Bobbi."

"We're not through yet," Brady began.

"I am," I said. "Either charge me or I'm going home after I speak with Mr. Klein."

Brady didn't like it. He shot me a look that said he'd slap me in jail in a minute if he thought he could get away with it. The fact that he didn't reminded me again of my connection with Erik Lundstrom. At that particular moment I had to admit I was damned glad to have it.

"Stay available," Brady growled and waved us off.

"I need to take care of something," Klein said as we left the squad room.

He led the way back to the front desk. A woman seated on one of the hard plastic chairs in a waiting area stood up when she saw us, said anxiously, "Harvey?"

"Ellen, this is going to take a while. I don't think you should wait."

"Have you seen Bobbi? Is she all right? What's happening?"

She was tall and slender with pale skin, light brown hair, and huge, prominent hazel eyes that burned with feverish intensity. She clutched a long, knitted navy jacket closed with a fisted hand, pulling the shoulder pads off-center.

"I don't know anything yet," Klein said, distracted, maybe a little brusque. "I'll call you when I do."

"But you won't have a car—"

"I'll take a cab. You should never have come with me, Ellen." A patient, forced tone. "Go on home."

She didn't answer, just stood there watching us as we walked away.

"My wife," Klein explained as he pushed open the door to a small interrogation room.

He'd compartmentalized his emotions, so he was functioning just fine, but I thought the effort was costing him something.

"Suppose you tell me what happened," he said.

When I finished giving him the story, filling him in on the lies I'd told Brady, he was quiet for a few seconds. Then: "How long have you known Bobbi? Ten hours or so?"

"About that."

He touched a faint, two-inch white scar near his hairline above his right eyebrow. "Bobbi and I were in Chicago at the Democratic convention, 1968. I know why I'd go to the mat for her. Why would you?"

I gave him a wry grin. "I've been asking myself the same question. Since you're old friends, I'd feel a hell of a lot better if you'd tell me you think I did the right thing."

"You mean do I think she could kill anybody?"

I nodded, wondering if he'd do a little judicious waffling.

"No, not a chance," he said.

"Okay," I said, relieved. "What about her relationship with Sandy?"

"What about it?"

I remembered Bobbi rambling on about how she'd promised Sandy the best attorney. Klein was a good guess. "You do know what the relationship was?"

"Yes. But I'm not going to tell you anything about it until I've spoken with Bobbi."

"Fair enough." I dug my card from my purse, which was lighter now because Brady hadn't returned my gun. "Give me a call, will you? I've stuck my neck out pretty far tonight."

He promised he would and thanked me. I left him there to wait for Bobbi.

Walking down the hall toward the front desk, I could see Ellen Klein sitting, hunched over with her arms wrapped around herself even though the temperature in the station wasn't really cool. As I approached, she recognized me, then looked past me for her husband.

"Harvey—is he finished?"

"No, he hasn't seen Bobbi yet."

No matter how exhausted I felt, I thought Ellen Klein was in a lot worse shape. Maybe for her, Brady might authorize a ride back to my van.

"Mrs. Klein, I'm Delilah West. I'm helping with Bobbi's case. Why don't you let me drive you home? There's really no point in your staying around here."

"Oh, no, thanks. I'm fine, just a bug of some kind. I have to wait and make sure that everything's okay, that Bobbi's okay."

"Are you sure?"

"Yes. Positive."

Well, I tried.

I could still request a ride from the desk sergeant back to the Garden View Apartments to collect my van, or ask to have my gun returned. But either appeal might summon Brady, so what I did was call a cab and get the hell out of there.

SHORTLY BEFORE DAWN, I had this great nightmare about waking up in a prison cell, the kind of dream that's so damned real you feel as though if you don't wake up, and I mean right now, you'll slide out of your world and into that other grim reality. Just my subconscious reminding me none too subtly of what I was risking by lying for Bobbi Calder.

An effort, but I snapped awake, breathing hard, a fine sheen of sweat slicking my body. The bedside clock read 4:48. The room was already ghostly gray with dawn light filtered through morning fog. I closed my eyes and settled back under the sheet, still exhausted. Three hours of sleep was not enough for the grueling day I was sure lay ahead.

My mind resisted drifting off, however. The harsh prison nightsounds seemed to echo in my head, and I could feel the thin, jailhouse mattress beneath my body.

At the time I lied to Brady, I'd felt as though I was stepping into quicksand, but I'd jumped right in without even looking for a handy tree branch to cling to. I remembered Harvey Klein saying *I know why I'd go to the mat for her. Why would you?*

Earlier, on the drive with Bobbi and Rita, I'd considered Bobbi's case from the standpoint of the money it would generate, and concluded that I couldn't afford to take her on. Of course I'd done a quick about-face, but the thought had been there, tainting my action. Add to that my major guilt trip because of the source of my own quick rise in fortunes, and bingo: overcompensation in spades.

I hoped to God that Klein was right about Bobbi's innocence. My gut feeling said he was. But the police already had means and opportunity. If they came up with a motive for Bobbi, my lies would be a mighty thin dam against the flood of physical and circumstantial evidence, and Brady would just love to get me for perjury and see us both go down. The only way to save myself and Bobbi might be to find the person who had killed Sandy on my own.

If that prospect wasn't daunting enough, there was one other question that haunted me, staying in my mind as I finally went back to sleep.

What if Bobbi really was the murderer?

BOBBI AND I made the morning paper. She was hot copy, a righteous politician booked for homicide; oh, how the mighty have fallen, don't you love it? I was "assisting the police in their inquiries."

After two reporters called in rapid succession around six, I'd shut off the phone and reset the alarm to give myself an extra hour's sleep, so by the time I got to work even the No Parking space next to the dumpster in back of my building was occupied. I had to find parking on the street four blocks away and hoof it, carrying the cheese danish I'd picked up at the minimart when I stopped to fill the gas tank on my way to work.

The marine layer had stayed offshore last night, so brilliant sunlight was already busily brewing auto exhaust into a fine chemical stew of sulphuric and nitrous oxides. My office is located near Orange County's Civic Center. The building's your basic stucco box, three stories high, put up in the sixties. I wouldn't be surprised if they tear it down one of these days and replace it with a monolithic gray highrise, the kind you see all over the county, the ones with more than a passing resemblance to a tombstone.

Inside, in the tiled entry, Harry Polk, the janitor, was industriously washing down a wall. Harry's a dried up little man with gray hair cut in a kind of butchered punk style and pale gray eyes. He's taken to wearing polyester slacks and limp white shirts, the thrift store kind, but at least a bit classier than his old white T-shirts and stained chinos. The interior of the building looks a lot better these days, too. I think Harry's worried that with my new class of clientele I'll look for other quarters.

He dropped his rag in the bucket and came running, fairly quivering with excitement. "Miz West, you okay? That fool paper said you was assisting the cops, but I betcha tracked that woman down yourself, didn't you, and caught her right in the act."

"Not quite, Harry. Miss Calder's my client, and I'm going to have to prove she didn't do it."

"Is that right? Well, you need help, anything at all, any time, you just let me know."

"Thanks, Harry. I'll remember that."

"Meantime, I'll just keep my eyes open, watch your back if you know what I mean. Can't be too careful."

This might sound like a dotty old man's rambling unless you knew about the fresh pink scar just below Harry's breastbone where he took a knife for me last year. Nothing like that was ever going to happen again, but I couldn't bring myself to burst his little bubble of self-importance, so I just said, "Right, Harry," and went on upstairs.

I've made one change in my office setup. I moved
down the hall to a two-room suite after Danny came
to work for me. He has the outer room, and I have
the inner one which works okay when he's there to
serve as receptionist. When he's not, I have to leave
my door wide open and hope nobody sneaks in and
rips off the computer. Not a real big risk, Danny
says, since these days nine hundred dollars will buy
one with a thirty-meg hard disk, whatever that is.

I started the coffee and gave myself fifteen minutes to drink two cups and eat my danish before I
checked in with Rita's service. My call quickly
brought Rita herself on the line.

"Where have you been?" she demanded. "I know
you didn't spend the night in jail. Matt checked."

I explained about the phone. "Sorry, but I was
beat."

"When I saw the paper, I couldn't believe it. What
happened?"

"I wish I knew."

"But Matt said you were there, at the scene."

It seemed Matt had checked things out pretty
thoroughly, easy enough for him to do since he was
on the public defender's staff.

"Rita, we need to talk about this," I said. "But
not over the phone. Do you have some time later?"

"I'll make time. When?"

I checked my calendar. I had two other ongoing
investigations and a meeting with Hiddev Corpora-
tion, the company name an acronym for high den-

sity development and their address in Newport's financial district in Fashion Island a guarantee that there'd be no problem with billables.

"Where will you be the rest of the morning?" I asked.

"At the gym."

"Okay. I'll try to stop by."

She gave me my messages—from Matt, who, according to Rita, was as frantic as she was to speak to me. Other callers included Sam Newley, five more reporters, and—surprise, surprise—Lieutenant Brady.

Just as I hung up, I glimpsed somebody coming into the outer office—Danny, shrugging off his backpack, calling, "Don't shoot. It's just me."

"Don't you have classes?"

"Nothing I can't make up."

He stopped in my doorway, leaning down to take the bicycle clips off his pant legs. Danny bikes to work and school and sometimes logs another hundred miles on the weekend, most of that in Southern California traffic. I tell him he's either the bravest man I know or the dumbest.

All that exercise leaves him whip thin, a fireball of energy, his dark eyes crackling with intensity. He wears his black hair long, but somehow it never gets mussed up by his helmet.

"I figured you could use some help, so I came on in," he said. "What have you got?"

I told him I was doing a background on an insurance fraud case and trying to locate an old guy's high school sweetheart. Some things we could track on the computer, but a lot of it still requires good old-fashioned digging.

"No reason why I can't go down to the Hall of Records," he said. "Just a matter of looking stuff up, right?"

"Well, yes, assuming you know where to look."

"Oh, I'll figure it out," he said cheerfully. "Trust me."

He would, too. Probably in about a tenth of the time it had taken me to learn. "Okay, it's all yours."

After he took off to retrieve his bike from Harry, who guards it faithfully in the storeroom downstairs, I had the last of the coffee and tried to decide who to call first.

The telephone rang, saving me that decision. It was Harvey Klein.

"Bobbi's been arraigned," he said. "I'm arranging bail, so she'll be out in a couple of hours. She wants to see you, Delilah. Her house in Laguna—around four? Can you make it?"

I said I'd have to let him know, hung up, and called my appointment at Hiddev to ask if it were possible to change our meeting.

"No, I'm afraid not." The warmth of our first conversation was gone, replaced by a definite chill. "You came very highly recommended, but since you're suddenly busy with—other things—" the in-

flection in his voice told me he'd read the morning
papers too—"you probably couldn't give us the in-
dividualized service we require."

"Probably not."

"Well, then, you'll understand if we call somebody else. We'll keep you in our files for future ref-
erence."

Sure.

Nothing like being fired before you're hired in the
first place.

I called Harvey Klein and told him there was no
reason why I couldn't meet with Bobbi in Laguna at
four.

FIVE

I STILL HAD my little list to tackle. I phoned Matt's office first, half hoping he'd be in court. He wasn't.

"So you finally surfaced," he said, pleasantly enough, but I could hear all the subtext, just as I could picture him: in his shirt sleeves, tie loosened, dark brown hair, always in need of a haircut, curling over his collar.

Matt prides himself on being fair, goes out of his way to be. It's one of the qualities I like about him, so why does it, at the same time, bug the hell out of me?

"One of the P.D.'s called first thing this morning to tell me what happened," he said. Subtext: *Why did I have to hear something like that from an outsider?*

"The good old grapevine."

"Has its uses. Did you get home at all last night?" Subtext: *Of course you got home, you sure weren't in jail. So why didn't you call me?*

"I came in pretty late. I just didn't feel like talking to anybody."

"I see. Understandable, I guess." Subtext: *I'm not just somebody. I'm the man who's shared your bed*

*off and on for the past year, so the least you could do
is pick up the goddamn telephone.*

"Oh, for Christ's sake," I said. "If you're pissed,
spit it out. I'm not in the mood for games."

"I'm not mad. I'm confused, maybe a little hurt,
and—"

"Mad."

"All right, damn it, yes. You get yourself in trouble and I'm the last one to know. Why didn't you call
me from the police station last night?"

"Matt, I didn't need a lawyer."

The wrong thing to say. I knew it the instant the
words left my mouth. And not even true, considering the string of whoppers I'd told Brady.

"Or a friend either, I guess," he said, sounding
terribly, mortally injured. "If you ever do, you know
where I am."

Click.

I CONTINUED my winning streak with Sam Newley,
who had a variety of things to say about unprofes-
sional behavior and conflicts of interest, none of
them good.

"Do you have any idea what kind of position this
puts my office in?" he demanded.

"No. What?"

"Intolerable," he snapped. "I told you from the
beginning I wanted absolute discretion. And what do
I get? This sordid mess."

He was mad at Sandy for having the bad taste to get herself killed, furious to learn that Sandy was connected to Bobbi, and particularly upset at me being mixed up in the murder. In a way he was right. If I'd followed my instinct and stayed away from Sandy's apartment . . . yeah, *if*.

I told him I was sorry and said I'd try and contain the situation as much as possible, a lame promise but all I could come up with.

"You do that," he said,

Click.

SINCE I HAD no intention of calling reporters, Brady was next.

"Just wanted to tell you myself that your client's fingerprints were on the murder weapon," he said. "And the victim's blood was all over your client's clothes. Oh, and one other thing, we got a witness says the two of them had a big argument the day before the murder."

"So what? People argue all the time."

"It was enough to get Miss Calder bound over for trial."

"An arraignment's not a verdict," I said.

"As good as, in this case. Why don't you play it smart, Mrs. West? When Roberta Calder called you, it was to tell you she'd just killed the Renkowski dame and beg you to do something to get her off the hook, wasn't it? If you change your statement right now, I'll get the D.A. to go easy on you."

"Nice try. Listen closely and you'll hear my answer."

This time it was my turn to hang up.

I CAUGHT UP on my calls from the day before and still made it to the Ultimate Fitness Health Spa by eleven. The spa is done in slick grays and blues with the latest in physical torture machines and a suspended hardwood floor for aerobics. A class was in session. I could hear the reverberation of a driving rock beat and an instructor yelling encouragement from the big room in back.

Rita, dressed in hot pink leotards and coordinated sweat band, was behind the health food bar, concocting a shake for two female bodybuilders who were taking a break from pumping iron.

"Hi, Delilah," Rita said. "Want some?"

"Only if it's made with ice cream and chocolate syrup."

It definitely wasn't. Rita poured the mixture into footed tumblers, a thin gray gruel that smelled of yeast. While the bodybuilders slurped up their treat, Rita waved over an assistant so we could retire to a glassed-in office to drink some mineral water while I brought her up to date on Bobbi's case.

I left out the part about my big lie. Rita's probably the best friend I have in the world, and I wasn't about to share any accessory-to-murder charge that might be coming my way. She's also too sharp for her own good.

"Wait a second," she said. "I gave Bobbi your business card, but how come she had your home number?" She stared at me. "What are you leaving out here?"

"Nothing you need to know."

"Something that can get you in the slam along with Bobbi, I'll bet." A sigh. "Okay, I won't ask. What can I do to help?"

"Tell me what you know about Bobbi."

She nodded, adding some mineral water to her glass. It crackled and fizzed on the ice. "Well, I'm afraid I don't know much. We're not close personal friends. I met her about a year ago at a fund-raiser— the Wildlife Federation, I think—and we hit it off. She talked to me about Slo-Grow, and I volunteered some time—not a lot, I'm stretched pretty thin with the businesses, but I do what I can. And Farley and I ran into her at other meetings."

They'd talked enough so that Rita knew something of Bobbi's background in the civil rights movement and her passion for protecting the environment. "Never anything about her personal life. She's very private. But I like to think I'm a good judge of character, Delilah, and I'm telling you Bobbi Calder would not stab another human being to death."

"Did you ever meet Sandy Renkowski at any of these functions?"

"No, I don't think so. There's usually a lot of people, though, so I can't be sure."

"And Bobbi never mentioned her?"

Rita shook her head.

So it would be up to Bobbi to fill me in on her relationship to the dead girl. If I got a move on I'd have time to stop for a burger and fries and do one interview connected with my insurance fraud case before I drove down to Laguna.

BOBBI LIVED on a street in Laguna that snaked along the crest of a high hill, an area called Top of the World. The house nestled beneath ancient live oaks and towering eucalyptus, built of wood siding and a shake roof so you had to assume there had been no brush fires in the area for a good thirty years. Even from the driveway the view of the city below, edging the Pacific, was breathtaking.

Harvey Klein answered the door. He'd taken off his suit jacket and undone his tie. His shirt, shadow-striped white-on-white, fit so perfectly it had to be custom-made.

I apologized for running late, citing traffic, then asked, "How's your wife today?"

"Better, thanks."

He wasn't. His baggy eyes were red-rimmed. He'd knicked himself shaving.

"And Bobbi?"

"Bearing up. It's one of the things Bobbi does best."

A trait they had in common, I thought, as he led me from the small entry hall into a sparsely furnished living room. Bobbi sat, drinking a cup of tea, on a huge sectional sofa that curved around one side of the room, her legs tucked under her. A slab of gray-veined white marble served as a coffee table. Bookcases covered the opposite wall, centered by a fireplace. The walls were white, the floor a polished pine. Hanging lamps did away with the need for end tables. Austere—no, just stripped of the nonessentials. French doors looked out on the ocean, thrown open to let in a warm, fragrant sea breeze.

Bobbi swung her feet to the floor, set her cup on the coffee table, and stood up. "Delilah, thanks for coming down."

Exhaustion and grief had pared her face down to bone and shadow. Her hair was damp, pulled back with silver combs, and she smelled fresh out of the shower. She wore faded jeans, a dusty pink, over-sized knit top; her long, narrow feet were bare.

"Bobbi, will you be all right now?" Klein tightened his tie and picked up his jacket, which was draped on one arm of the sofa. "I really should get back to the office."

"You go ahead," Bobbi said. "I'll be fine."

Klein said good-bye to me, then Bobbi excused herself and walked him out, linking her arm with his. I could see them in the hallway, the way he held her tightly for a moment, Bobbi a good two inches taller, leaning her head down against his shoulder.

She saw me watching.

When she came back, she said, "Given time, old lovers make the best friends."

And old lovers' wives? Surely Ellen Klein must know about Harvey and Bobbi's past connection. Still, Ellen had seemed genuinely concerned last night. I wondered if I could be so tolerant in the same situation. I also wondered how many more secrets Bobbi had.

"Would you like some tea?" Bobbi asked.

"No, thanks."

"It's cold anyway." She sat back down on the sofa, gesturing for me to join her. "Were you ever in jail, Delilah?"

"Oh, yes. Once or twice."

"I never get used to it."

Her voice had a dry, remote quality. She'd gotten herself firmly in hand, and I'd bet she'd done it through pure willpower. I couldn't see any symptom of chemical stablizers.

"Good thing you could make bail," I said.

A wry grin. "One of the advantages of owning Orange County property free and clear. Harvey told me what you did for me. I can't imagine why after our meeting yesterday."

"Impulse. A hunch. Everybody tells me you couldn't possibly have killed Sandy. Did you?"

"*No*—God—" She jumped up and went over to the bookcases. An open shelf held a collection of framed pictures. She brought one over and handed it to me.

I recognized a younger Bobbi, hair tumbling free to her waist. She stood with another young woman, their hands clasped, and in turn each holding one hand of the little girl who stood in front of them.

Bobbi pointed to the child and said, "Sandy." She set the picture on the marble coffee table and stared down at it.

"I met Lynne in Selma when Sandy was two years old. Lots of times Lynne would bring Sandy on the marches. Not to Selma, of course. Sandy stayed in Chicago with Lynne's mother. In the sixties you were—what? In grade school?"

I nodded.

"Unless you lived through that period you can't possibly know what it was like. There was a bond so strong it still links all of us—most of us—even today. But with Lynne and me the bond was special. We became like sisters."

"Has she been told about Sandy yet?"

"Lynne died of breast cancer six years ago."

I murmured that I was sorry, the word woefully inadequate.

"Sandy was in her last year of college when it happened," Bobbi said.

Sandy finished school and went to Boston because that's where her father lived. Her parents had not been married, and they had split up when Sandy was an infant, so she'd never seen much of her dad. "I guess she felt an urge to get closer if she could. She gave it a good try. She even took his last name, but I don't think it worked out. A cold Boston cod, Lynne always called him."

So Sandy had come to California a year ago, living with Bobbi for two months until she found the apartment in Santa Ana and a job with an insurance company. I recalled from my background check that she'd left that job to go to work for Supervisor Newley, but I hadn't turned up her stay in Laguna.

"You were close to her?" I asked.

"I didn't see very much of her while she was growing up, but she was Lynne's child, and we had our own special connection. Now she's dead. My God, I can still see her face and that knife in her back—the blood—"

She broke off, shivering. Outside, the marine layer had moved back in, bringing an early fog. The wind was suddenly sharp and chill. She got up and went to close the french doors.

"They're going to convict me of killing her," Bobbi said. "Maybe it's only right. What I said last night—it *was* my fault. I'm to blame as surely as if I had stabbed her myself."

"Why is that?"

"Because she went to work for Sam Newley."

"Look," I said. "I know you cared for Sandy. I'm sure you were horrified when she was arrested, but to somehow connect her death back to Newley—"

"Of course it's connected," she said fiercely. "Sandy never stole anything."

"We subpoenaed the bank records, Bobbi. She made deposits to her account that equaled the thefts. She had marked money in her possession when she was arrested."

"Anybody can deposit money in a bank. All you need is an account number. And tell me, did you see her take that money from the incoming envelopes and put it in her purse?"

"No." During my stint undercover, I'd narrowed down the possibilities to Sandy, but I'd never actually seen anybody steal anything, which was why I'd agreed with Vero's idea of planting the marked money. Suddenly I remembered Sandy's face staring back at me through that patrol car window.

"You think it was a setup?" I asked.

She nodded.

I could see how it could happen, just the possibility making my stomach contract with sick fury. I could also see that Bobbi Calder might be totally paranoid. I knew she wasn't fond of Sam Newley, but then neither was I. The basis of my dislike was purely intuitive. I had the feeling, however, that her animosity went a lot deeper.

The other thing I could see quite clearly was that if Sandy had been framed for stealing the money, she wasn't the only person who had been set up.

I had been, too.

SIX

Outside, wisps of fog drifted against the windows. Gloom filled the room. Bobbi switched on a hanging lamp. "I could use a drink. How about you?"

I nodded. Definitely a drink. Maybe two or three. I said I'd have what she was having, vodka and tonic. She brought over two tall glasses. I took a good long swallow before I said, "Okay. Let's hear the rest."

"When Sandy lived here with me, she helped out with Slo-Grow. After she went to work with the insurance company, she came down when she could. And she heard me talk, God knows, always on my soapbox," she said bitterly, then hunched silently, staring down into her drink.

"You can't change the past, Bobbi, no matter how badly you want to."

"I know that, but it doesn't help." She looked up, her eyes haunted. "There's a hard core of us in the county who form a kind of think tank. It's a little like the military trying to outplan the enemy. We were right here in this room one night, brainstorming. Sandy was here. We all think Newley's in line to head up the Board of Supervisors. And I said, 'Oh, if only I were a little mouse in Sam Newley's office, the things I could tell.' Sandy got the idea then, but she didn't say a word to me. She just called me up a week later and said, 'Squeak, squeak, Bobbi. Guess where I am?' "

"She went to work for Newley to spy on him?"

Bobbi nodded.

"She was working there when we began hearing rumors that the County Board and the Planning Commission had approved an immediate development startup in the canyon."

I remembered the finale of that abortive coup. The Slo-Grow group had been out in force when the bulldozers arrived, yielding that memorable photo of Bobbi facing off the big machine, the protest sparking a public outcry that forced the county to reconsider.

"Sandy told you what was about to happen," I guessed.

"Yes."

"And then Newley found out about Sandy?"

"He denies it, but he must have. I thought you were the one who linked Sandy back to me, so you can imagine how I felt when Rita insisted that I meet you."

"All right," I said. "For the sake of argument, assume Newley found out about Sandy's little Mata Hari act. A simple firing seems sufficient. Why go to this elaborate frameup to get rid of her?"

"Because it wasn't about Sandy, Delilah. He was out to send a message to me."

"Okay, say you're right about Newley setting Sandy up—"

"I am right."

"Say you are. A nasty little setup is one thing. Murder is something else. There was damn good evidence to convict Sandy. I can tell you that. Why would Newley want her dead?"

"I don't know. God, I never imagined he hated me so much, that he'd go this far."

She jumped up and went to the bar, fumbled a few ice cubes into her glass, splashed in straight vodka.

"The irony of the whole thing is that now the son of a bitch has bagged me, too," she said.

"You think he arranged it so you'd be blamed for killing Sandy?" I asked, wondering if all of this really was just paranoia, and how far she would go.

"Oh, no, he got lucky there. I set myself up on that one." She lifted her glass in a mock toast. "Here's to lucky ol' Sam and the rest of the meateaters of the world, damn their souls to hell."

She drank deeply, leaning against the edge of the bar for a moment. Alcohol and fatigue were going to do a double whammy on her pretty soon, and we had a lot more things we had to discuss.

"Why did you go to Sandy's apartment, Bobbi? Why did you argue with her the day before she died?"

"How do you know about the argument?"

"The police know about it. Brady just couldn't keep from gloating. My guess is probably a neighbor." And maybe the same person who called the police last night, somebody I definitely wanted to talk to.

Bobbi took her drink over to the window and stood, looking out at the lights coming on in the canyon below, dimmed by the gray fog.

"Sandy'd been raised on the stories, you know. Me and Lynne. All the others. Selma, Montgomery, Washington. It must have seemed so important, maybe even glamorous. I think she wanted to prove herself our equal, to do something that counted."

But Sandy hadn't counted on being arrested and going to jail, to facing a prison term. And there were no brothers in arms for her. She was all alone. No wonder she went into a tailspin. She holed up in her apartment, keeping her answering machine on, not taking Bobbi's calls.

"I finally went over there," Bobbi said, "the day before she died. I tried to persuade her to come here and stay with me, to reassure her that if she didn't want Harvey to handle her case, we'd get somebody else, the best lawyer in the country. We'd prove she was innocent. She wouldn't listen. She got more and more upset.

"She told me I was a fraud, Delilah, that we were all frauds. We'd spent our nights in jail, holding hands, singing, knowing damn well nothing serious was ever going to happen to us." She pressed her forehead against a square pane in the door. "She was probably right."

"Bobbi, I want you to think carefully. Did she say anything else—about anybody she was having problems with?"

"I don't think so—no."

"Did she have a boyfriend? A lover?"

She turned to look at me, hesitating a moment, then shaking her head. "I never met one, and we never talked about things like that. Too busy discussing the big, important issues," she said grimly.

"All right, now what about yesterday? Why did you go back to see her?"

"She called me. She left a massage on my machine, kind of strange and rambling. It scared me. And then I couldn't get through to her."

"Do you still have the recording?"

"I don't know—yes, I think so, because when we got home today, I noticed I hadn't reset the machine."

Her Code-a-Phone sat on the end of the bar, the green message light flickering. Bobbi's eyes filled with dread as I rewound the tape and pressed Play.

"Bobbi, it's me. There's something else—it can't wait. I have to tell you, so call me. Call me right away." Sandy's voice sounded tense, frayed, and terribly alive.

Bobbi made a wounded noise, deep in her throat. "Oh, God, if I'd come home a little earlier—if I'd gone up there right away—"

She tossed down the rest of her drink and set the glass on the bar. "Is there any chance you can find out who killed her for me?"

"I can give it my best shot."

"Then do it. Not just to get me off. To make sure he pays for what he did."

"Are we talking about Sam Newley again?"

"I want you to tell me that."

"How did you come to hate him so much?" I asked.

"You see what he is. Isn't that enough?"

What I saw was that she'd evaded my question.

"There's one other thing," she said. "I know this is going to sound pretty heartless, but I have to bring it up. You lied for me, so you could be in a lot of trouble if the police find out. Do you have somebody to take over the investigation in case they do?"

"No. But if you like, I'll certainly be glad to refer you to another investigator, somebody who wasn't stupid enough to risk a felony charge by lying for you."

"God—I'm sorry." She sounded a little sick. "I really do appreciate what you did. I feel responsible, just as I do with Sandy."

An abject pause—waiting for me to say I understood, I suppose. I might have said that Brady would pull the records at the phone company, so my lie was a delaying tactic, and that afterward I'd probably come up with something else. But that meantime, maybe, Brady wouldn't think this was an open-and-shut case. He's a pretty good cop, even if he is a cold-hearted bastard. If he's got one little doubt, he might keep on looking.

I might have said all those things, but I didn't. To hell with relieving her mind. A sliver of pain gouged my left temple. My eyes felt gritty from lack of sleep.

"All right," I said. "What's it going to be?"

"You—if you'll still take the case."

I nodded.

"One last thing," I said. "The letter bomb threat. Do you think Newley's mixed up in that too?"

"I don't know. I doubt it. Plenty of people don't like me threatening their paychecks, and some of them aren't too nice about telling me so. I really just think it was a nasty prank."

"I'd still like to take a look at it."

"Okay. Come on."

She led the way down the hall to her office, taking care, I thought, to put one foot precisely in front of the other.

The messy room contrasted sharply with the rest of the neat, uncluttered house. A desk and several folding tables jammed the space, all overflowing with boxes of files and correspondence, piles of printed fliers. Environmental posters and a few pictures filled the walls, one of the pictures a group photo of the Slo-Grow volunteers. Along with Bobbi, I picked out Harvey and Sandy.

Bobbi opened a desk drawer and handed me a nine-by-twelve mailing envelope, stiff with card-

board inserts. Her name and address were printed in
large block letters, written with a black, wide-tipped,
permanent marker. No return address. Postmarked
Anaheim. Some oily dark smudges on the brown
paper.

Inside was a triggering mechanism attached to fine
brass wire but, luckily for Bobbi, not to anything
that might provide guts for the bomb. There was
nothing else in the envelope except a note written in
the same block letters, which read: YOU WERE AL-
MOST DEAD.

I handled the envelope and its contents carefully.
If the person who sent it was a pro, there would
probably be no prints, and God knows how much the
thing had already been handled, but no sense taking
chances.

"So, it's a joke," she said. "Isn't it?"

"I wouldn't be laughing if I were you," I said
grimly. "You should report it to the postal authori-
ties. It's sure to fall under some federal jurisdic-
tion."

"Me call in the Feds? Not likely. With my record,
I don't think they'd feel too kindly toward me, especially when they know I've just been charged with
murder. You handle it."

"Okay." I tried to think of what I knew about letter bombs. "But, meanwhile, don't take any more
chances. Any packages you get, any kind of envelopes that are stiff like this or full of paper, anything

more than regular correspondence, don't open it. I'll take this and have somebody look at it.''

She found a small mailing carton for me to stow the envelope in, moving wearily. Shadows under her eyes looked like old bruises.

We went back to the living room so I could collect my purse. It sat on the floor next to the marble coffee table. I picked up my glass and the picture of Bobbi and Sandy and Lynne as well, tidying up, returned the glass to the bar, and went over to put the picture back on the bookcase.

Up close now, I could see the rest of the photo gallery there. A few were sepia-toned, people in turn-of-the century clothing, old cars. A man in a uniform stood next to a World War Two vintage fighter plane. Children. More pictures from the sixties. A whole history on those shelves. I'd started to turn away when a group photo caught my eye.

I could pick out Bobbi and Lynne. No Ellen, but the short man beside Lynne with long hair and a beard, wearing bell-bottom jeans—Harvey Klein, it had to be. It was the man standing next to Bobbi who gave me a jolt. Rangy, tall, his moustache a wispy Fu Manchu, his shoulder-length hair already beginning to thin, his arms wrapped possessively around Bobbi.

I'd only met the man a couple of times, but I knew him all right. My client, Sam Newley.

I looked at Bobbi.

Gotcha.

"Old lovers," she said softly. "They also make the worst enemies."

SEVEN

I DIDN'T KNOW much about letter bombs, but I knew somebody who did: Wayne Loftland, retired for medical reasons from the Orange County Sheriff's Department after fifteen years of service, ten of those on the bomb squad.

First, though, after leaving Bobbi Calder, I headed inland to hole up in a Black Angus until the northbound traffic subsided. A massive construction project on the Santa Ana Freeway adds more frustration and delays these days. No, thanks.

The restaurant's bar area looks like an oversized barn, but the booths are secluded and dark. No windows, just lots of dark ersatz wood and dim lighting. Perfect place for a rendezvous with your lover if you happen to be on speaking terms.

I just wanted someplace quiet to get my thoughts in order and have a decent meal. While I waited for a table, I called Wayne. His wife said he was off refereeing a Little League game, but he'd be home in a couple of hours, that I should come on by, they'd love to see me.

I planned to check in with Rita, but the hostess called my name, so I decided my messages could wait.

No, I didn't want a cocktail, I told the waiter. I still had a mild buzz from the vodka and tonic I'd had with Bobbi. I sipped iced tea and confronted my anger, which was still simmering at a slow boil.

So Bobbi had been ungrateful. Well, who had asked me to stick my neck out? And so she was keeping secrets. Everybody does. Some are just buried more deeply than others. And in my business if you expect people to be honest with you, your ass can wind up in a very painful sling. Call it guilt; call it stupidity. I'd gotten myself into this mess so I'd damn well better figure out how to get myself out.

Over salad and warm, coarse-grained bread, I put my mind to looking for some pattern in the events swirling around Bobbi and Sandy. By the time I got my end cut of prime rib, I felt as if I'd been staring at a Rorschach inkblot for half an hour.

Bobbi had not been about to tell me any details about her old affair with Sam Newley or how they came to be enemies. All she said was: "He talked a good game, but when it came right down to it, all Sam cared about was Sam."

Obviously Sam Newley had gone on to the reality of money and politics while Bobbi stayed the sixties idealist. If the original passion between them had been volatile enough, I could see it flare up into a pretty explosive feud. Given the vindictiveness Bobbi portrayed, if he had found out about Sandy being planted in his office, I could believe—maybe—that he'd cooked up the scheme to frame her using me as his cat's paw, but murder? Sandy may have uncovered all kinds of development shenanigans, and she may even have been calling Bobbi and me to spill the beans the day she died. Still, in my experience, politicians can weasel their way around almost anything, so why would Newley take such a risk to silence her?

I passed on dessert, but took an iced tea refill. Too bad my beverage didn't come with the tea leaves, because I was getting nowhere with my musings.

What I had to admit was the possibility that the murder was totally unrelated to Sandy's job. In any homicide, family, lovers, and friends top the list of suspects. It did not escape my notice that this put Bobbi up near the head of the line. I hadn't turned up a boyfriend during my original investigation for Newley, which, I remembered now, had surprised me.

I stirred my tea, staring down at the swirl of ice, and considered my reaction. My surprise about Sandy's lack of a boyfriend hadn't been just a routine expectation that a beautiful young woman would have a love life. I really had *assumed* she was in a relationship.

During my two-week stint as a temp in Newley's office, Sandy had never actually mentioned a boyfriend, never talked at all about her personal life. I remembered a couple of other women giggling about this attorney or that sales rep, women's room talk, but Sandy hadn't joined in. Neither had I. Not because I wasn't interested in men, but because I already had one man too many in my life.

And there had been another minor incident: Sandy hunched over her desk one morning looking miserable, looking as though she'd been crying, as a matter of fact, and one of the other women tilting her head toward Sandy and saying knowledgeably, "Man trouble."

The woman didn't know this for sure, you understand. I know because I pried. I get paid for prying. No, she was operating on intuition the same as I was.

So that was the sum total of the basis for my assumption about a boyfriend for Sandy. Not a hell of a lot in the cold evidentiary world of the law, and Bobbi had been no help. Still, deeper digging was necessary. My original investigation hadn't turned up a lot of things, so there might have been any number of jealous, whacked-out persons of either sex in Sandy's life.

The only thing left to consider was the bomb threat.

There's a theory that everything in life is connected. Following that logic, the bomb threat could be tied to Sandy's death; how directly was another matter.

Bobbi was probably right. The nine-by-twelve envelope with its ugly message was from a kook, and any connection with Sandy was purely metaphysical.

All I could do was start following trails to see if they all ended up in the same backyard. I'd begin with the bomb threat tonight; tomorrow I'd start backtracking Sandy's movements, filling in the gap between the time she'd argued with Bobbi and the time she began calling us, and, along the way, zeroing in on her personal life.

I wasn't sure how I was going to find out if Sandy and I had been set up for that theft in Newley's office. I wasn't even sure if I could *ever* nail down that slippery little sucker. Assuming Bobbi's suspicions were true, I'd bet there were very few people involved in the frame, loose lips being a universal problem. Tony Vero, Newley's assistant, had my nomination for head carpenter.

First impressions can be dead wrong. Boy, do I know that from experience. Nevertheless, I still get them, and my first reaction to Vero was that he was too handsome and too smooth. He had black hair, shiny as a crow's wing, olive skin, and dark, dark eyes so opaque you'd never get a glimmer of what was going on back there in that cold, sharp brain.

Oh, he could have arranged things for Sandy and me. I had no doubt of that. On Sam Newley's instructions my background checks had specifically excluded him, a fact that bothered me at the time, but I chalked up my concern to a personal distaste for the man and reminded myself sternly that Newley was the client. Anyway, my investigation had quickly picked up Sandy as the thief, so there had

been no need to check out Vero. Now I wanted to
know everything about him fast.

Signing the charge slip for my meal, I had a sobering moment wondering for the first time in
months if the money was going to be there to pay my
Amex bill when it came in. Somehow I was going to
have to find a way to juggle my time so I carried
enough caseload to keep up a cash flow. Thinking
that, I realized I'd committed myself to finding Sandy's killer, even though I thought that I was probably a damn fool for doing it.

Well, what choices did I have? I could crawl under the covers and hide, or I could find out if I'd
been responsible, even inadvertently, for Sandy's
arrest and maybe her death. Which meant I really
had no choice at all.

On my way out, I checked my service. No calls
connected with the Calder case; nothing I couldn't
handle tomorrow morning.

My eyes were adjusted to the dark restaurant;
outside, I blinked and squinted in a last glorious
blaze of evening sunlight. The fog was still over on
the other side of the coastal hills.

Heading down the freeway on-ramp, I could see
the whole sweep of the Santa Ana range off to the
east, dominated by the twin peaks of Saddleback
Mountain. Housing tracts were filling up the valley
right to the base of the peaks and traffic at El Toro
Y, that convergence of the Santa Ana and San Diego
freeways, was still backed up at seven o'clock P.M.

The land inside the Y has already sprouted two highrise office buildings, with more to come. About the only thing blocking the total development of the area is the big chunk of property occupied by the El Toro Marine Air Station.

The mountain peaks were clearly delineated now, shaded in blues and purples, a sight becoming rarer. With all those people and all those cars, the south county's postcard landscape vanished more and more frequently behind a pall of smog.

Maybe we natives figure that things like bad air and earthquakes are the price you pay for paradise, and take our beauty when we can. That's just what I did, lowering the window of the van as I drove north, savoring that clarity of light and perfection of temperature that can only happen in southern California.

When I arrived at the Loftlands', Peggy said that Wayne was out on the patio having a beer, go on out and join him. Yell when we were through talking business, and she'd bring out coffee and devil's food cake. We could all have a visit.

On the patio, Wayne sat on a lounge chair, sipping a Bud Light. He looked tanned and fit, almost back to his old stocky weight, relaxed and cheerful in khaki shorts and a Garfield T-shirt. His springy brown hair looked sun-bleached and his nose sunburned.

"Hey, Delilah—" He didn't get up, gestured to a cooler with his beer can. "Want one?"

"I'll pass this time."

"Take a load off," he said.

I sat down, and we spent a few minutes playing catch-up. I told him that business had been going well. He said he was spending a lot of time with his two kids, almost as much relandscaping the backyard.

"It looks terrific," I said.

He'd created a stone-lined stream bed, dry now, that meandered through grasses, wildflowers, and shrubs, the foliage looking silvery in the fading light.

"All native plants," he said proudly. "No sprinklers. Strictly drip irrigation."

"You're feeling okay then?"

He held out his hand. Not exactly rock steady, but a hell of an improvement over the uncontrolled tremors he'd had as he hovered on the edge of a complete breakdown.

"Not too bad for a guy who played with dynamite for ten years," he said. "What do you have for me?"

I'd brought along the carton that held Bobbi's bomb threat. I handed it over. "It hasn't been printed yet. Outside's probably a bust, but I'm hoping we may get lucky with something on the inside."

He nodded, got up, and switched on a porch light; then he removed the manila envelope carefully, opened it, and studied the contents. "Nice," he said, reading the note.

"Is it a hoax, or did the person sending that know what he was doing?"

"Oh, yeah, he knew all right," Wayne said. "The cardboard's nice and stiff. That's essential for the real thing because you can't have any flexing. See this firing pin? When it's loaded for bear, it's under spring tension with about an eighth of an inch slack. Add some HE, shotgun primer, and a dynamite cap, and ka-boom!"

"What kind of explosives?"

"If you had a big box, you could use maybe black powder or, hell, a stick of dynamite, but this small? It has to be plastic explosives. C-4, that's the putty stuff, or Flex-Ex, which is flexible sheet explosive."

"There doesn't seem to be a lot of room in there." I indicated the thinness of the envelope. "Can it hold enough to do a lot of damage?"

"Damn right. A couple of ounces shaped into a small cylinder, say the size of a ballpoint pen, I guarantee it'll really make your day. I hope you advised your client to start screening her mail."

"I did."

"Good. Because—see this?" He pointed to the smudges on the outside of the envelope. "Plastic explosives have an oily base. You handle this stuff, you can get it on your fingers, or on your gloves, 'cause if you're smart that's what you'll be wearing. Then say you touch the envelope. The stuff can come off and leave a stain—like this."

I feel the hair rise on the back of my neck. "But there were no explosives in the envelope."

He shrugged. "Maybe there were. Maybe your bomber had a change of heart—this time."

He put the envelope back in the box and returned it to me. "All I can tell you is don't call me if your client gets another one like this. Call the bomb squad."

"Most of the ingredients you mentioned sound pretty simple," I said. "But plastic explosive—how easy is that to acquire?"

"Easier than you think. Oh, you can't get it off the shelf at Home Club, but it's around."

"Would somebody in land development have any legal use for it?"

"You mean like for blasting stumps or boulders? No way. You blast a big rock with C-4 and you know what you get? Millions of little-bitty rocks flying around at thousands of feet per second."

"So no commercial use."

"Damn little. Now take a guess who would be the prime source."

I thought about people whose chief function was blowing up the planet. "The military?"

"You got it. Not the sole source, of course. There are explosives dealers. You should be licensed to buy from them, but, hey, money talks. Then you have your terrorist groups—Middle Eastern, the IRA. They got enough stockpiled to vaporize half the free world. If he needs the cash, a dealer's principles get a little vague."

"Hey, you two," Peggy called through the screened patio door. "You about ready for dessert?"

"Delilah?" Wayne said.

"That's it for now."

"We're finished, hon," Wayne told his wife. "You want some help?"

"No, I got it."

We went inside for the cake and coffee because the sun had set, and the air grew quickly damp and chill as the first tendrils of fog drifted in. After we finished, Wayne walked me to the door and gave me a good-bye hug.

"Thanks for answering my questions, Wayne," I said. "Send me a bill on this one."

"Nah. Professional courtesy, or call it a payback. I sure as hell owe you a few, not to mention what I still owe Jack. How long has it been now? Six years?"

"Six and a half."

Days go by now when I don't think of Jack at all, then suddenly something like this happens, and my heart feels as though a hole has opened up.

"I miss him," Wayne said.

"Yes," I said. "Me, too."

I INTENDED to go straight home, but I found myself driving the opposite way, toward Huntington Beach.

East, over the mountains, stars still shone, but were quickly winking out as high streamers of cottony fog moved in.

On the Coast Highway, the moisture was a fine gray mist, just beginning to shroud the streetlights. The tourists and the beach bunnies had fled, leaving a few stalwart souls to huddle around fire rings the way Jack and I used to do. I could almost taste the strong, salty, fishy odor of the sea.

Not long ago 400,000 gallons of Alaskan crude poured out from the punctured hull of a tanker off shore, closing the beach with a tide of oily muck. By now the dead birds had been carted off, and most of the oil cleaned up except for stray globs that would wash in for years to come.

Go home, Delilah. Jack's not here.

I drove south instead, memories flooding in.

Jack dying on a cold January night on a cliff overlooking the sea, dying in my arms while his blood soaked into the sand.

I pulled over somewhere north of Laguna, cut my lights, and sat, staring blindly across the highway toward the ocean, searching for a happier memory.

Our wedding day in my dad's house in Altadena. I'm upstairs in my old room, five minutes from show time. I've ordered my attendant away, but she keeps knocking to remind me of the time. I've snagged both pairs of my white panty hose, the lace dress I bought for fifty bucks in the garment district looks as though it belongs on a wide-eyed choir girl, my

*little crown of orange blossoms is making me sneeze,
and what the hell am I doing anyway?*

A knock, then Jack sticks his head in the door.
"Hey, anybody in here getting married today?"

"Look at me. Do I look like I'm ready for this?"

"Darlin', you look absolutely beautiful . . ."

Bright headlights shone full in my face, startling
me back to reality, and I realized two things: that the
convenient place I'd chosen to park was the turnoff
to Erik Lundstrom's private road, and the headlights belonged to Erik's Lamborghini.

EIGHT

THE LAMBORGHINI blocked my path, so there was
nothing I could do but sit there as Erik got out and
came over to look in at me, astonishment on his face.

"Delilah?"

The headlights shone on sandy hair that was turning prematurely silver. Too dark to see the color of
those blue, blue eyes, but no matter. I remembered
exactly what they look like.

"Sorry," I said. "I didn't realize—I mean, I just
needed a place to stop for a minute."

"Are you all right?"

"Fine. If you'll back up a little, I'll get out of your
way."

"You're sure you don't want to come up to the
house—"

"No. No, really, it's late. I need to go home."

"Okay," He hesitated, added: "Delilah, you can
stop here any time. I want you to know that."

He went back to his car, his tall, hard-muscled
body casually elegant in slacks, a leather bomber
jacket, shirt open at the throat.

God!

I got the hell out of there and drove home as fast
as possible.

ANOTHER LATE NIGHT and damn little sleep. Making an ass of yourself will do that. No sense wondering why I'd parked in that particular spot, deliberately crossing the highway to do so with a more convenient shoulder open for miles along my side of the road. I'm sure a whole psychology text could be devoted to the subject.

I'd been attracted to Erik from the moment we met, no doubt about it, and still was. After tonight, how could I deny it? Maybe that attraction had undermined my relationship with Matt from the beginning. At some point, I supposed I'd have to come to grips with my feelings for Erik, but not now. I needed a clear head to deal with the Calder case. A few zee's wouldn't hurt either.

Busy coping with embarrassment and insomnia, I forgot to check my calls.

Not good.

Next morning behind my office building I wedged the van into a space meant for a compact, and never noticed the brown Chevy with official plates.

Definitely not good.

Inside the building, through a big glass door, I could see Harry waving frantically. I decoded his semaphoric signals as an enthusiastic greeting, but when I got inside, he whispered loudly, *"Cop,"* and I looked up to see Lieutenant Brady lurking at the top of the stairs like a bulky gray shadow.

"Good thing I caught you," Brady said placidly, looking down at me. "Saves sending out a patrol car."

"You want me to come up with you?" Harry scowled at Brady.

"No, Harry, I'll be fine."

"Well, leave your door open. And holler if you need me."

I said I would and headed upstairs.

"You do have your protectors," Brady said, amused.

"I guess it's my helpless qualities." I led the way to my office, unlocked the door, invited him in, and made nice, offering coffee, which he refused.

The message light was blinking on my phone. "Excuse me," I said. "This will only take a minute."

The service reported I'd had several urgent calls from the same person: Brady.

Hanging up, I said, "Sorry about that. I just now found out that you wanted to speak to me."

A thin smile. "Yeah, you're good at getting calls only when it's convenient. About that one you said you got from Bobbi Calder—funny thing, the phone company has no record of it being placed from the apartment."

"Oh? Well, I never said it was, did I? I don't know where Bobbi placed the call, lieutenant. Maybe she went out and used a pay phone."

"Went out? This is the same woman who's too hysterical to give you any kind of details about what happened?"

I shrugged. "People do strange things when they're in shock. I don't mean to rush you, lieutenant, but if that's all—"

"It's not all. Seems you left out a very interesting tidbit the other night, Mrs. West. Did you really think I wouldn't dig up the fact that you were the one who got Sandy Renkowski arrested?"

"No, of course not. It's a matter of public record."

"Which you didn't see fit to share with me."

"Look, my part in Ms. Renkowski's arrest was purely coincidental, a separate incident entirely. It had no bearing on her murder."

"So you wouldn't mind coming down to my office and making a complete statement about this little coincidence?"

"I'd be happy to." I glanced at my calendar. "Say, midafternoon?"

"Say one o'clock and if you're not there, I send a squad car." He stood up and looked down at me with grudging admiration. "I have to hand it to you, Mrs. West. You're a helluva good little tap dancer. One thing though. Keep it up long enough, you may just miss a step and fall flat on your face."

"I'll keep it in mind."

I fixed a pleasant smile on my lips until he was out the front door. He'd no sooner cleared the threshold before Harry was there, scanning me anxiously for rubber hose marks.

"You okay, Miz West? He didn't try no rough stuff or nothing?"

"No, he knew you were around, so he was a perfect gentleman."

"Yeah, well I'm thinkin' maybe I oughta rig up some kinda signal in here." He was no longer content to use his old system that had me banging on the heat register. "Maybe like an intercom. I seen these things on TV. You put 'em in a baby's room, so you can hear the little tyke when he wakes up. I figure that couldn't cost too much."

No, I didn't want him to rush out and buy one on his lunch break, but I promised I'd think about it. Anything to send him back downstairs so I could get some work done.

After I started the coffee, my first call was to Bobbi to tell her about my talk with Wayne Loftland. I relayed his opinion about the contents of the manila envelope as bluntly as possible.

There was a small silence on the other end of the line, then Bobbi said, "All right. You've scared me." She promised to warn all the Slo-Grow volunteers, to personally scrutinize all the mail, and to call the police if anything looked suspicious.

"I'm going to need a list of any people who have a grudge against you or your organization, Bobbi. If you have a hate-mail file, I want that too."

"I don't keep that garbage," she said. "And I'm not going to write up an enemies list. Not now."

"Bobbi—"

"*No*. You've warned me, and I'll take precautions. Meanwhile, the important thing is to find out who killed Sandy, and that's what I want you to concentrate on."

I sighed. "Your decision."

No sense bringing up my philosophical musing about connections. She wouldn't buy it for a minute. All I could do was hope we'd get lucky and find a print on the envelope. I told her I would need a list of all the volunteers and anybody else she could think of who knew Sandy.

"You mean here in California?" she asked.

"I mean anybody, anywhere."

"Well, I don't know anybody back in Boston except her father. Her grandmother, Lynne's mother, is still alive, but she's in a nursing home in Chicago in the final stages of Alzheimer's."

"Maybe a college roommate. A girlfriend. Or a boyfriend. Past or present."

"I'm sure Sandy had lots of people in her life, but I'm afraid I don't know them."

"Her father then. Have you spoken to him?"

"Yes, a little while ago."

"Is he coming out here?"

"No. I thought he would. *I* would if my daughter was lying in that—that—" she couldn't say morgue, said instead: "that place. He said as soon as they release the body—that's how he said it, the body—a local funeral parlor would take charge and ship it back east for burial. He also said he assumed I wouldn't be allowed to leave the state, and he was damn glad of that so there wouldn't be any possibility that I would try and attend the funeral."

"He doesn't know the facts, Bobbi. He only knows you've been charged with his daughter's murder."

"Yes, like a lot of people," she said. "Quite a few of them have called to tell me what they think of me."

"It'll only get worse. You might think about changing your number."

"I'll be damned if I will," she snapped.

"Screen your calls then." I looked longingly at my Mr. Coffee. The water had dripped through the grounds and the office had filled with the fresh-brewed aroma. "Do you have Mr. Renkowski's number handy?"

"Hold on. I'll get it." She came back in a second, read off a number with a 617 area code, and supplied Stanley as a first name. "Oh—and, Delilah? I mailed you a check—a retainer." She mentioned a generous sum. "When you need more, just let me know."

"Thanks," I said politely. "And don't worry. If I wind up in jail, I'll refund the unused portion."

"Okay, I deserved that. Are we even now?"

"More or less. I'll be in touch."

I knew I wasn't up to talking to Sandy's father without a cup of coffee. After two cups I still wasn't ready, but I dialed the Boston number anyway. All I got was the housekeeper, who wouldn't give me Stanley Renkowski's business number, wouldn't be pumped, and only with a great deal of coaxing finally admitted he might possibly return for dinner at some unspecified time.

After that the mail arrived, and then I checked the files Danny had left on my desk. Neat, dot-matrix printouts listed most of the things I needed to wrap up the insurance company case. As for old Mr. Tilson's high school sweetheart, Danny had found out that Mildred Drake had married one Walter Quincy thirteen months after graduation, July, 1941. After that there was no record of them living in the L.A. area.

Now what? Danny wrote.

I scrawled a reminder that we'd had a little run-in with the Japanese later that year, so Walter Quincy's service records might be a good place to check. I told Danny where I'd be at one o'clock and added: If I don't check in by four, send the cavalry. Then: P.S. Start backgrounds on Anthony Vero and Sam Newley. More later.

I knew I should call Harvey Klein and fill him in, but the morning was racing past. I fielded two calls from prospective clients, then hurried off to drop Bobbi's mock letter bomb at a private lab to be printed. After squeezing in a hasty lunch, I went on over to spend a lovely afternoon with Lieutenant Brady.

By the time he cut me loose, I didn't feel as though I'd been tap dancing. My feeling was more like the aftermath of a highwire act performed without a safety net below.

The only good thing I could report was that I hadn't thought about Erik Lundstrom more than about fifty times all day.

NINE

MAYBE I SHOULD have waited until the next day, but I was already in the area and there was still some time on the old office hours meter, so what the heck. After checking in with Danny, I decided to combine a little fishing expedition with a courtesy visit to inform my ex-client, the County Supervisor, that my promise to "contain the situation" was now in the dumper.

My news did not make Newley's assistant a happy man.

Newley was off at a County Board meeting, so it was just Vero and I in his office adjoining Newley's, the room almost as large as the one belonging to Vero's boss and expensively furnished with sage green carpet, black leather furniture, and lots of chrome. Something that looked like an original Georgia O'Keefe hung on the wall, but then what do I know about art?

A scowl spoiled Tony Vero's classic Armand Assante face. I could even detect a little flicker of annoyance in those smooth, black eyes. He was smartly dressed as usual in a charcoal gray suit with the faintest mauve pinstripe, which matched his shirt.

"What I don't understand," Vero said, "is why you were working for Ms. Calder in the first place. It's a clear conflict of interest."

"I'd call it more of an unfortunate coincidence." Not easy, but I tried for a neutral tone in my voice. "I had already completed my assignment here, and I had no idea of any connection between the two women. I was retained by Roberta Calder on a completely different matter."

"Nothing to do with Sandy Renkowski?"

"No."

"Well—" He hesitated, picked up a silver letter opener, put it down, evened a stack of files that were already aligned. This wasn't the first time I had noticed his stumpy hands and spatulate fingers, but they always surprised me, like seeing a toad's feet grafted onto a gazelle. He immediately lowered his hands out of sight.

"I still don't understand why you were in Sandy's apartment."

I gave him my official lie. "Bobbi called in a panic and asked me to come."

"And you went?"

"Yes."

"Knowing this was something to do with Sandy?"

I nodded.

"Because if you knew, I mean, the smart thing to do was stay away."

"I suppose that's what you would have done."

"Damn right," he said.

"Keep in mind that at that point I didn't know about Mr. Newley and Bobbi's—well, you know—about their *past*." I leaned forward, ready to discuss all the juicy tidbits.

He blinked, but not before I saw startled speculation leap in his eyes. He hadn't known about Sam and Bobbi's old affair, I'd bet on it.

"So it has turned into a bit of a mess," I admitted. "It's all so bizarre. Sandy working here as a mole, then being accused of stealing from the park fund—"

"*You* were the one who pointed the finger at her," he said.

"Oh, I haven't forgotten that. Not for a minute." *Or the fact that you probably engineered the whole thing.*

"Well, let me remind you. The work you did for us is privileged information."

"Ordinarily that's true, except that in a murder case client privilege pretty much goes out the window." So much for my halfhearted stab at smoothing over client relations. My heart wasn't in it. "There's another complication. Bobbi Calder has retained me to look into Sandy's murder. And Bobbi has this theory: She thinks Sandy never stole anything from the park fund, that somebody in this office set the whole thing up. So what I'm wondering, Tony—did you frame Sandy for the theft?"

Anger erupts from most people. Vero just turned solid and stony cold.

"Okay, that's it," he said.

"I couldn't ever prove it, you understand," I went on. "Even if you admit it, it would be my word against yours. I'd just like to know if you did it."

He stood up, and he didn't try to hide his ugly hands. They were clubbed into fists as he strode around the desk.

"Out," he said. "Now."

"I'll take that for a yes." I got up and headed for the door, pausing to add, "One mistake you made, Tony. You used me to do your dirty work."

IT WAS FOUR-FOURTEEN and I was taking a chance on catching Sam Newley, but I was *still* in the area and now my adrenaline was up, so I slogged over to the County Building.

The Board of Supervisors' meetings are unpredictable. They can drag on all day unless something important comes up, like a ribbon-cutting ceremony or a golf game. I got lucky. The meeting was still in progress.

A bailiff said to give it another half-hour, sounding like he knew just how to gauge these things. He did. I slipped into the crowded chambers to listen to the droning discussion of the budget, paper clips and rubber bands being the central topic, and did a quick dimout until thirty-five minutes later when a gavel banged, bringing me out of my reverie.

I waited by the door, watching Sam Newley. He worked his way through the crush of people, stopping to shake a hand here and there, trailed by a beefy man with an overflowing briefcase.

Newley had gained a few pounds since Bobbi's photo was taken, some of it sagging over his belt, and lost a lot more hair. A few long wisps were combed to conceal his balding crown. He flashed a smile so loaded with sincerity you just knew that it was donned in the morning along with contact lenses and an old school tie.

At the door, Sam clasped the beefy man's hand, said: "Let's talk about this ASAP. Call my office. We'll get together." And he was off, leaving the man with his mouth open.

I pulled a flanking maneuver, skirting the mob, met up with Newley as he exited the building, and said, hello.

"Mrs. West?" He broke stride for a moment, then kept walking at a fast lope toward the parking lot, forcing me to hustle to keep up. "I'm in a hurry. Was there something you wanted?"

"Just a minute to talk."

"Make an appointment." He didn't slow down, and he didn't waste a smile on me.

Since I was through doing subtlety today, I said, "I know about your history with Bobbi Calder."

That stopped him. He halted in front of a long row of cars. Behind him late afternoon sunlight glinted off a sea of glass and chrome.

"I'm sure Bobbi couldn't wait to fill you in on all the juicy details," he said bitterly.

"Actually, she said very little."

"Then why are you going out of your way to ambush me like this?"

"Because I wanted to ask you about Sandy. How soon after she came to work for you did you suspect she was spying for Bobbi?"

A dull red tide of anger swept up his throat and over his face. "I resent the implication in that remark, Mrs. West. Bobbi called me up with her half-baked accusations after the girl's arrest. She even accused me of sending her a bomb scare."

Ah, Bobbi. Another thing you forgot to mention.

"Did you?" I asked.

"*Jesus*—it's bad enough listening to that crap from Bobbi. I sure as hell don't have to take it from you. You're fired."

He stalked off down the row of cars. I stayed on his heels. "I finished my job for you, Mr. Newley. You can't fire me. What about it? Did you set Sandy up for that theft charge personally, or did you have Vero do it? Didn't it mean anything to you that Sandy's mother was once your friend?"

He stopped next to a black Jag in a corner marked with RESERVED PARKING signs. He'd clamped a lid on his anger, but I thought he might put a few scratches on the Jag's sleek surface the way he was jabbing the key and missing the lock.

"All that sixties crap," he said. "We were a bunch of undisciplined, know-it-all kids out to change the world. Bobbi's trouble is she never grew up. My so-called vendetta is all her imagination.''

"She didn't imagine Sandy's murder. Or do you think Bobbi really did it?''

"Not the Bobbi I used to know. But people change, and you find they're capable of almost anything.'' He finally got the door open, paused. "One thing, Mrs. West. If you think I'm going to forget any of this, you're mistaken. I have a long memory. Just keep that in mind.''

Yeah?

So maybe his vendetta with Bobbi wasn't simply in her head after all. I watched him as he climbed into his Jag, slammed the door, and drove off. He still hadn't answered any of my questions about Sandy.

THE INSIDE OF THE VAN felt like a sauna, so I started the engine and turned on both air conditioners, front and rear, while I called Danny from the car phone.

"Want your messages?'' he asked.

I didn't, not really, but I sighed and said okay.

He listed Bobbi, who'd just left word that she was sending the list I'd requested; Harvey Klein; another prospective client; and Rita. No Matt, which was just as well considering my encounter with Erik last night.

"How far did you get with the backgrounds on Vero and Newley?'' I asked.

"Newley was easy," Danny said. "Lots of stuff put out by his PR department. And, of course, there's plenty of newspaper articles. I just got started on those. Vero's going to be tougher. Do you want what I have? I can drop it at your place on the way home."

"That would be great, Danny."

"I'll come in for a couple of hours tomorrow morning and see what else I can dig up."

I realized suddenly that it was Friday. Danny normally didn't work weekends. "Are you sure? You're not getting behind at school?"

"Last final this morning," he said. "Summer session doesn't start for a few weeks."

"*Finals?* Why didn't you say something?"

"What's to say? I think I did okay."

Which meant he probably aced them.

"So I'm all yours," he went on.

We had talked about his working full time a while back when money was plentiful and I figured I could use all the help I could get. I didn't know how to break the news to him that my situation had changed.

"Oh, and—Delilah?" he went on. "If you have a cash flow problem, don't worry about it. I know you're good for the money."

"Jeez, what are they teaching you in those business courses?" My voice sounded a little husky, probably because of the gigantic lump in my throat.

He laughed. "Dirty Tactics 101 comes next semester. Will you be in tomorrow?"

"I'm not sure. I'll call you."

I made one more call, to Harvey Klein. His secretary said he was in court. I left a message asking if he would set up a time tomorrow for me to get into Sandy's apartment.

The time I spent on the phone put me in the thick of traffic. My condo was only a short jump by freeway, that is if you traveled sometime around midnight. Right now the freeways had turned into elevated parking lots, so I maneuvered my way across town on surface streets, which was only slightly faster.

After a half-hour of creeping along smelling exhaust fumes, a Coco's restaurant looked like an oasis in the Mojave. I joined the crowd of rush-hour escapees, waited my allotted twenty minutes, and settled in with some overseasoned pea soup and undercooked sirloin.

Well, hell, I deserved it.

THE INFORMATION on Vero and Newley was waiting when I got home, as Danny had promised. I wanted nothing more than a shower and about ten hours of sleep. My eyes felt gritty and my body ached with fatigue, reminding me that I was now well past thirty years of age, that the big four-o loomed, and a sufficient amount of rest was required.

I promised myself only another half-hour of work, took the file into my living room, sat on the sofa, propped up my feet, and reached for the telephone, groaning as I remembered I had planned to call Sandy's father. It was eight-fifteen, which meant it was eleven-fifteen on the east coast. Better wait until morning.

So Rita first for a brief update, and then I dialed Harvey Klein's home number. Ellen answered on the first ring. When I told her who I was, she said, "Oh, yes, from the police station. Listen, please, can you tell me how things are going? Harvey won't say anything. Playing lawyer—you know? And I get a little crazy worrying about Bobbi."

"Haven't you talked to her?"

"Yes, sure, we've talked, but it's all so awful—"

I heard the rumble of a male voice in the background. Then she broke off and put her hand over the mouthpiece, I guessed, because their voices became muffled, but I know the sound of an argument when I hear one.

Then Harvey came on, a thread of restrained anger weaving through a harshly remote tone. "Delilah? I'd appreciate it if you didn't relay anything confidential to me through anyone, not even my wife."

"Of course," I said. "That goes without saying."

"Yes, well—I didn't mean to accuse you of anything. I'm afraid I tend to be overly cautious about these things."

"I understand. No problem. Now what about getting into Sandy's apartment? You got my message?"

"Yes. I set it up for nine o'clock tomorrow morning."

Somebody from the police department would meet the two of us there. When I asked about the autopsy report, he said he only had the preliminary, which established that Sandy had been stabbed to death at approximately six to seven on Wednesday evening. The D.A. expected to have the full report sometime next week. Harvey would request that the coroner's office send me a copy.

"Bobbi told me what you found out about that letter bomb threat," he said. "My God, it scares the hell out of me just thinking about it."

"I hope it scares Bobbi into being careful."

"I think it did," he said. "Any possibility you can trace who sent the thing?"

"Truthfully? I doubt it. Anyway, Bobbi doesn't want me to follow up on it. She wants me to devote my time to Sandy's murder."

"Any progress?"

"Well, I managed to piss off Sam Newley and his assistant. Otherwise, nothing to report." Twinges down my neck and across my shoulders reminded me that I planned to cut this short. "Listen, I'm beat. Can we continue this tomorrow?"

"Sure," he said, sounding relieved and more than a little beat himself. "See you in the morning."

I didn't open the files on Newley and Vero after all. I skipped the shower, put on my jammies, set the alarm for 6:00 A.M. and went straight to bed.

Although I was exhausted, falling asleep was another matter. I lay there, thinking about patterns and connections.

Sam and Bobbi; Bobbi and Sandy; Bobbi and Harvey; Harvey and Ellen.

Gidget and Moondoggie.

Me and Erik . . .

TEN

WHEN THE ALARM jarred me awake the next morning, I got right up and called Stanley Renkowski—for all the good it did me.

The housekeeper advised me that he would not come to the phone and that he was not interested in speaking to "any of you people in California" about his daughter.

I said, "Would you please tell him I think they have arrested the wrong person, and that I'm trying to find out who really killed Sandy?"

A little silence, signifying, I hoped, that she was thinking it over.

"Please," I said. "Go tell him that. I'll hold on."

She came back two minutes later. "He says he already knows who killed his daughter and not to bother him any more."

"I just have a few questions," I said quickly. "Maybe you could tell me—"

"No, ma'am. I won't tell you anything."

She hung up.

Well, if I had to, I could get on a plane and go bug Stanley in person; meanwhile, telephoning looked like a lost cause. I thought longingly of crawling back into bed, but I knew better. If I fell asleep again, nothing less than the seismic jolt of California's Big One would get me up.

I showered, dressed, and went to Mom's for breakfast, taking along the files on Newley and Vero to read while I plowed through a platter of eggs, bacon, sausage, and home fries that was designed for two truckers to share. I knew all this food would require a double session tomorrow at the Ultimate Fitness Health Spa, but it was worth it.

Between visits from my old friends who work at Mom's and shoveling in the calories, I scanned the information Danny had put together.

Samuel Thomas Newley had been born in 1941 to the Beverly Hills Newleys (oil, cattle, and orange groves), got his degree in political science at the University of Chicago, received a commission as an officer in the Marine Corps in 1968, served four years. He married Marjorie Anne Cummings of the Baltimore Cummingses (shipping and dry goods), had two children, headed up Newley Development Inc., until he was appointed to the Orange County Planning Commission. Power playing was to his liking, so he ran for the Board of Supervisors.

Danny had copied a bunch of recent newspaper stories about Newley. Supervisor Sam with Governor Duke Deukmejian, with Dan Quayle, with the statue of John Wayne being installed at the Orange County Airport, playing golf with his good friend, Colonel George Raeford, who was in charge of public affairs at the El Toro Marine Air Station.

Wayne Loftland's comment about the military as a source for high explosives came to mind, of course. What also struck me was how familiar a man's public face could be and how you still knew diddley about what went on inside his head and behind his front door. As for that young man in Bobbi's picture with his long hair and Fu Manchu moustache, I had a feeling he had vanished long ago.

I sighed, stuffed the material back in the file, and glanced at the brief sheet on Tony Vero, which included only the man's vital statistics and current address. Then I indulged in one last cup of coffee and went to say adios to Jorge Sanchez and the kitchen help.

MOST SENSIBLE PEOPLE were sleeping late, so the traffic was light and I was going to arrive at Sandy's apartment early. With time on my hands, I got a sudden yen to cruise by Tony Vero's place. I didn't have a whole lot of time, certainly not enough to do any serious harassing. I merely wanted to reconnoiter, to check out the enemy turf.

The fog had vanished early, leaving bright, hot sunlight, which meant we were in for a day of scorching, smoggy heat. I took a jump on the 55 freeway to the Orange Hills where bulldozers were chewing their way through the strip of backcountry fronting the Santa Ana Mountains. Vero lived in the first stage of a new townhouse complex. The builder,

I noted, was Newley Development, Inc., and wasn't that a happy coincidence?

The complex looked like something Picasso might have dreamed up after a drunken week in Santa Fe, the blindingly white cubes topped with blue tile and shaded by newly transplanted, full-grown palm trees. I had just circled past Vero's unit when his garage door slid open. I slipped into a guest parking slot next to a Volvo, wondering if Vero would notice me, getting more of a charge than is probably healthy out of the fact that it was likely he wouldn't.

I heard the throaty roar of an engine, all wrong for the BMW I could see in the garage, and then I saw why as a motorcycle rumbled out, something big and black and powerful. Even I know a Harley when I see it. The rider wore a leather vest over his T-shirt, torn jeans, scuffed boots, and short gloves on the ugly hands, with holes cut out on top of the fingers. No helmet, so there was no mistaking that it was Tony Vero who roared past me, unshaven, with a faded blue bandanna tied around his head.

Well, well, Tony.

More than likely this biker getup was all for show, but I would have loved to tag along and see where Vero was going. Not that there was a chance of following the motorcycle in my van through Orange County traffic. Just to remind me of this fact, everybody was now up and out on the 55 freeway where the traffic didn't seem to flow so much as come to a frenetic boil, much of it beachbound and ready to party.

Because of my detour, I had gone from being early to being ten minutes late when I reached the Garden View Apartments. Harvey wasn't there yet either. The patrolman assigned to play watchdog waited on the wood walkway outside number 24D, frowning at his watch and sweating steadily. He was young and tanned, with sun-streaked brown hair. I knew without asking that he'd rather be on his way to the Newport Wedge than standing around waiting for me.

Good thing he wore a little plastic nametag or I'd never have known who he was. His tag said RON DICKEY. I identified myself and suggested we go on inside out of the heat to wait for Harvey, but Officer Dickey reminded me irritably that Harvey had the paperwork, and I wasn't going anywhere without paperwork.

This really didn't bother me too much, because now that I was here, I wasn't all that anxious to enter the door with the placard that read: CRIME SCENE. DO NOT ENTER. The memory of three nights ago was too fresh, of standing pressed up against the doorjamb with my gun drawn and fear cold in my stomach, of finding Sandy dead on the floor.

I had only a few steadying moments before I heard footsteps on the wooden stairs and saw Harvey climbing slowly up, looking as though he didn't want to be here either.

"About damn time," Dickey muttered. He said a curt, if civil, hello to Harvey, scanned the paperwork, then unlocked the door and ushered us in.

I thought about the cat bolting out the other night, and wondered what had happened to it, distracting myself, I suppose, from the purplish stain on the light beige carpet. Those neat white chalk outlines of the body are only for visual effect in the movies. Some masking tape indicated where Sandy had lain. The broken lamp had been removed; otherwise the room looked the same, although I assumed the carpet would have been vacuumed and everything gone over carefully.

Harvey made a little noise deep in his throat. His skin was the color of old ashes. Harvey, usually so elegantly turned out, looked as though he might have slept in the rumpled brown slacks and blue-and-white striped knit shirt.

"You okay?" I asked.

"Fine," he said harshly.

Officer Dickey made a show of folding his arms and leaning against the wall by the front door, and reminded us that we were to put things back where we found them and not to remove anything from the premises.

We didn't find very much, and even the sense of Sandy's presence seemed canceled out by Dickey's attitude and Harvey's anxiety. On the kitchen counter was a receipt left by the police that noted the things taken: a butcher knife used as the murder weapon, the rest of the knife set in a wood block holder, Sandy's address book.

There were two pictures on the nightstand in the bedroom in one of those double frames that opens like a book. Sandy with her mother, this Lynne older and much more somber than the woman in the photo with Bobbi. Sandy with an unsmiling, square-jawed, older man that had to be Stanley Renkowski. Everything else that was personal was put away out of sight in a dresser drawer: a few photos that I guessed were from her college days, canceled checks, paid bills, spare house and car keys, the detritus of modern life.

It seemed to me there were messages encoded in the neat rows of clothes in the closet, in the tangle of laundry on the closet floor, in the small kitchen, but I wasn't getting a thing, so I nodded when Harvey said, "Seen enough?"

As Officer Dickey let us out, I kept my hand closed around the shoulder strap of my handbag—and around the spare key to Sandy's front door that I had palmed from the drawer in the bedroom.

I followed Harvey down to the parking lot. Dickey clomped down behind us, headed straight for his patrol car, and vamoosed. In the sunlight Harvey looked even grayer and grimmer.

"Are you all right?" I asked.

"No, but I will be. I guess it just hit me in there—the way she died. I mean, I knew, but I couldn't imagine—sorry. You said you had some questions, but can it wait till Monday?"

I now had other fish to fry, so I said Monday was fine, remembering only after he drove away that I had failed to ask if he had the name of the witness who reported the argument between Bobbi and Sandy. Maybe I would find out for myself, but one thing at a time.

The parking stalls were about half empty. Sandy's car still sat under the stumpy eucalyptus, collecting dirt, stray leaves, and pollen. The tree was in blossom, with big globs of blooms alive with bees. The parking lot was quiet enough so I could hear their heavy drone over the distant laughter and splashing from the pool out front.

I went back up the outside staircase with a purposeful stride, hoping I looked as if I was supposed to be going into the apartment and that the neighbor who had probably already called the cops twice wouldn't see me and try for a lucky third shot.

Once inside, I detuned that part of my hearing that wanted to listen for sirens. If the cops came, they'd arrive Code Two, fast and silent, the better to catch me in the act. I walked slowly through the three small rooms, trying to feel the shape, the sense of Sandy Renkowski. Sandy alive that last morning. Getting out of bed. Showering, eating, putting on slacks and the pink blouse that would be sliced and bloody after the killing blow.

Sandy with the killer. Somebody she knew, or at least somebody she had let in willingly. There was no sign of forced entry.

They go into the small kitchenette. Sandy doing the social thing, offering tea or coffee, perhaps. The other person following. The wood block with the set of knives in sight on the counter.

Since there wasn't a lot of blood spattered around the apartment, I saw the scene like this: The killer grabs the knife with the largest handle, the butcher knife. Sandy turns and sees it. Her eyes widen in terror, her heart thunders. She turns and tries to run, but the knife plunges deep into her back. A lucky accident, perhaps, the knife turned flat and sliding in between the ribs instead of glancing off the bone. Or a professional, knowing where to put the blade.

Sandy staggers a few steps, arms flailing, hits the lamp and knocks if off the table, falls. Splotches of blood on the sofa, the coffee table, and a side chair, so the murderer must pull out the knife there, drawing it up to send the blood flying, then stabbing Sandy, already dead or certainly dying, over and over again...

I shivered and pushed away the gruesome scene. Back up. Think about what happened before the murder.

I knew she'd called me and Bobbi. Had she called anybody else? The police were sure to pull her current phone record. The defense had a right to disclosure of evidence, so I made a mental note to have Harvey request the record, along with the address book on the evidence list.

Meantime, I went through her bills and copied down the numbers she'd called for the last six months. Handy now that Pacific Bell itemizes, as well as charges for, every call made outside a local zone. There were no love letters, nothing so obvious, but I did find a brand new silk teddy, lavished with lace, the tags still attached. And inside a floppy tote bag in one corner of the closet, hidden by dirty clothes, I found another teddy, a silk robe, and a purse spray of Joy cologne. A wastebasket yielded a round compact of Enovid with all the pills punched out.

Of course there was no way to know how long the bag had sat there or if the contents had ever been used. Enovid may be prescribed for other reasons than contraception. I was pretty sure, however, that my feeling about the boyfriend had been right. I would have been happier at having the theory confirmed except for the fact that the bag was something the police would be likely to take. Finding it there in the closet told me that either Brady hadn't been all that thorough or that he wasn't looking for a lover because he was happy to tag Bobbi with the crime.

I put everything back where I had found it, including the key I'd swiped, and left the apartment, pushing in the lock on the door knob and hoping that nobody would notice the deadbolt was open. There were ten apartments on this back side of the U-shaped wing, five up and five down—nine not counting Sandy's. I began knocking on doors. Only two occupants were home, or at least answered my knock. Neither admitted to knowing Sandy or having seen or heard anything on the day Sandy died. Neither was among those I'd interviewed in my original investigation. Neither gave me more than sixty seconds before they shut the door in my face. So much for finding the witness.

It was now past lunchtime, and my farmer-sized breakfast was beginning to wear thin. The voices out in front by the pool increased in volume, singing a bawdy version of "Ninety-Nine Bottles of Beer." I put on my sunglasses and trudged around to join the party of seven people, a small crowd for a weekend.

One person remembered me. Whether it was the giddy heat of the sun or the copious amounts of Dos Equis being drunk, I was not only made welcome but instantly surrounded. I was offered a beer, a bathing suit, a male lap to sit on. I took the beer. Sure they knew Sandy, or most of them did. Not very sociable, but "a real fox; what a bummer." This from one of the guys I had met on that earlier foray while employed by Sam Newley.

Almost everybody was at work the day Sandy died, but one woman volunteered that she saw Sandy driving out of the parking lot around noon. Somebody else said he thought Sandy was home at three. He remembered because her damn cat was meowing outside her apartment door, and then it stopped—which it never did until Sandy let it in.

"Her cat," another woman exclaimed, a redhead among the California blonds. "Her poor little kitty. What happened to it?"

"I don't know," I said. "It ran out that night."

"Oh, the poor kitty—"

"Think I saw it," a man said. "Or one like it. Hit by a car down the block. Flattened."

"Oh, oh." The redhead began to weep.

An instant pall descended. People looked around uneasily as she wept. Murder is an exciting conversation piece, a dead cat something else again.

I finished my beer, left a handful of cards on a table just in case anybody remembered anything else once they dried their tears and sobered up, and went home.

EVEN I GET TIRED of restaurant food, so I stopped at the grocery store, laid in some supplies, and microwaved a diet pizza for lunch.

I thought longingly of the pool in my own complex. Beer is not allowed, but on the weekends it's crowded with sleek, glistening bodies. Like Sandy I didn't want to socialize. I just wanted to swim.

Instead I took the portable phone over to the couch, sat down, and extracted from my purse the list of telephone numbers I'd copied from Sandy's phone bills. I worked backward, the most recent calls first. Several numbers I recognized right away: Bobbi, Stanley Renkowski, Harvey Klein's office. I began dialing and turned up Domino's Pizza, One

Hour Dry Cleaners, a dentist, and two answering machines with female voices that chirped back the number and invited me to leave a message.

One long-distance number had been called twice. The operator advised me the exchange was in Glendale, Illinois. The reverse directory said the number was listed in the name of Gayle Thurber. Gayle was actually home.

I told her I was a friend of Sandy's, that Sandy had mentioned her to me, that if she hadn't heard what happened I hated to be the one to tell her, but—

"I heard," she said. "I just can't believe it. I was just talking to her a couple of weeks ago."

"Sandy told me how you knew each other. College, wasn't it?"

"We grew up together. Next-door neighbors."

Oops.

"Yes, right," I said. "Now I remember. It's so awful about Sandy. I needed to talk to somebody who was close to her, you know? And she didn't have a lot of close friends out here."

"Well, we weren't all *that* close," Gayle said. "Not any more. I'm surprised she mentioned me."

"Old friends are always best," I said. "Sometimes when we need to confide, why we just naturally turn to them. I'm sure she told you all about the trouble she was having."

"Trouble? No, not a word."

"No?" I tried again. "Well, I can understand that. She hated to discuss it. She usually just wanted to talk about happy things. Like her boyfriend."

"Sandy had a boyfriend?"

"She didn't tell you about him?"

"No, she didn't."

Gorgeous late afternoon California sunshine poured in my condo windows. There were sure to be some eucalyptus trees outside in bloom, full of bees. I knew for a fact that there was a swimming pool within walking distance, full of young, tanned bodies. People having *fun* while wasting their time.

"Would you mind telling me what you and Sandy *did* talk about?" I asked.

"The reunion," Gayle said. "Glendale High. It's our tenth, and I'm handling it."

"Look," I said wearily. "Disregard anything I've said to you. It was mostly lies. I'm a private detective investigating Sandy's murder."

"You *are*?"

"Yes. So if she said anything to you about her personal life, it would help a lot if you told me about it."

"Well, sure," Gayle said. "I'd be glad to help you if I could, but all we talked about was the reunion. You're really a private detective?"

"I really am."

I asked a couple more questions, but Gayle was truly another dead end. I hung up and declared myself officially off duty.

Too twitchy to sit still, I went for a run in the heat, cooled off in the crowded pool, considered making a salad for dinner, but went instead for Chinese takeout.

My fortune cookie read: YOUR LIFE IS ABOUT TO CHANGE.

About bloody time, I thought.

I needed a break, both in my personal life and on the case. Something. Anything.

I should have remembered that other old Chinese saying that's never placed in fortune cookies: Be careful what you wish for.

ELEVEN

ON SUNDAY I paid for my sin of gluttony with another run and a trip to the health spa, where I doggedly served my time on the stair climber, the exercise bike, and the weight machines. Then, showered and virtuous, I went to sip Evian with Rita in her office and give her a synopsis of what I'd been doing—everything legal, that is.

"Not a hell of a lot, is it?" I said.

"You just got started."

"I suppose."

We sipped some more water.

"Farley and I had dinner at Casa Maria's last night," Rita said casually. Then she paused, and the weight of the pause told me this wasn't a casual comment at all. "We ran into Matt." Another little hiatus.

I waited.

"Oh, nuts," Rita said. "I shouldn't even bring it up, but he was with somebody."

"I see."

"He introduced us. Angela something."

"Angela Ruiz."

"You know her? He said she worked in his office."

"We've met."

And Matt had a perfect right to have dinner with a fellow public defender, even if she was one of those women who manage to be willowly and voluptuous at the same time. Even if it was a Saturday night and I was home alone eating take-out Chinese.

"I shouldn't have told you," Rita said unhappily. "Me and my big mouth."

I assured Rita it was okay, really, although I'm not sure she believed me.

Driving home, I realized now that I'd had my flash of jealousy, I wasn't upset. If anything, I was sad and maybe even relieved. Matt was a good, honest, kind person who deserved somebody who would appreciate those qualities full time. But why the hell did she have to be as beautiful as Angela Ruiz?

Later, eating dinner alone for the third night in a row, I felt adrift and a little bit sorry for myself. I have plenty of friends I could have called. Any of them would urge me to come right over, but I'd bet by this time they were all pretty sick of cheering ole Delilah up.

Work is the best antidote for the blues, of course. I resisted, having promised myself a whole day off. Still, one quick phone call to Harvey, that's all. I needed to ask him to push the D.A. on those disclosure items. After my second trip through Sandy's apartment, I really wanted a look at her address book.

Ellen Klein answered and said that Harvey wasn't there. "Is it important, Mrs. West? I might be able to reach him."

"No, it can wait. Just have him call me at home. And please, call me Delilah."

"All right. Delilah? I have an idea. Harvey should be back any minute. Why don't you come over? Have a drink with us. I'd like that, and I'm sure Harvey would too."

I wasn't so sure he would, but my calendar wasn't exactly crowded tonight, whereas Monday looked to be a real killer. I decided to risk Harvey's displeasure and took her up on the offer.

THE KLEINS LIVED in a section of Irvine called Turtle Rock, in a big ranch-style house on a huge hillside lot. I counted three houses on their street with commercial-sized dumpsters out front and yards full of cement mixers and piled with lumber. Homes around here were twenty years old now. Their value had skyrocketed to the point that it was a good investment to do major teardowns.

Ellen came to the door in a white gauzy dress two sizes too big, belted in at the waist but drooping at the shoulders. When I asked about Ellen earlier, Harvey had said she was better. She didn't look better. In fact, she looked worse. The colorless dress bleached her skin and her ashy brown hair was dull and frizzy.

"I'm so glad you came." She gave my hand a squeeze, her long, pale fingers surprisingly strong. "Harvey's still not here. Come on in."

She led me into a family room with a view of a dark patio and a pool where moonlight glittered on the water. The room was good-sized, but there was too much furniture: a sofa and two loveseats in a flowery print, a full complement of cherrywood tables and brass-based lamps, and a whole wall of built-in cabinets in the same dark fruitwood, fronted with glass doors. Collections of figurines crowded the shelves—Lladro, Dresden, Hummel—enough china dolls to people a small town, plus plenty of birds and doggies for them to play with.

A squat tumbler sat on the coffee table with about an inch of colorless liquid in it. It might have been water, but I'd bet it wasn't. Ellen's hazel eyes had an alcoholic brightness, and her tracking was just a little off as she detoured over to pick up the glass and then navigated toward a wet bar in the corner.

"What can I get for you?" she asked.

A bit sloppy, but she got most of my drink in the glass and made a pass at her own tumbler—vodka and undiluted. So now I had a good idea what plagued Ellen Klein, and it wasn't a virus.

She waved toward the sofas. "Please—make yourself comfortable."

"Where is Harvey anyway?" I asked.

"At Bobbi's, I think—I mean, I'm sure he's there. They have so much to discuss. The case—everything—'' She sank down on the big middle sofa and took a gulp of her vodka. "I wish he'd tell me how it's going—really going, I mean. But Harvey won't talk about it. And I bet he told you not to say anything, didn't he? I don't know why he makes such a big deal about it. I'd just like to know if there's another suspect—for Bobbi's sake—can you tell me that much?''

"I don't know what the police have." I took a loveseat, kitty-cornered from her, and sipped my drink. "If it helps, I'm developing my own list of suspects.''

"You are?''

Maybe my expertise did not promote much confidence, because the news didn't seem to make her feel much better.

"I am," I said. "But that's all I can say about it.''

I wanted to ask how well she knew Sandy, but that would really be violating Harvey's mandate not to discuss the case.

"Did Harvey say what time he'd be home?" I asked.

"Not exactly. Sometime soon. I really am glad you came, Delilah. You were so nice the other night at the police station and then on the phone. With Harvey's schedule we don't see many people.''

There was resentment in her voice, normal enough considering the fact that her husband was off offering solace as well as counsel to his ex-lover. Of course

I could also put myself in Harvey's shoes. The man probably had good reason to stay away.

I made sympathetic murmurs about how rough Harvey's workload must be on her.

"It's worse now with David gone," she said. "Do you have children?"

"No," I said.

"David's at Harvard. He's going to be a lawyer like his father. They're very close."

She tossed off enough of her drink to bring the level back down to an inch, studied the glass, and said, "How 'bout a refill, Delilah?"

She had just the tiniest problem with the *L*'s in my name now, and some trouble pushing herself up from the overstuffed cushions, but she was holding her liquor like a pro. I got up quickly and said, "Let me do that for you."

I took her glass and made sure there was plenty of water added to the vodka.

"David could've had his pick of schools," she said. "He could've stayed out here."

"Hard to beat Harvard."

"Especially—" trouble with those *L*'s again. "'Specially the location. As far from California as you can get. He's working back there this summer too."

"Kids have to lead their own lives," I said. "Look at the sixties. You and Harvey and Bobbi. Imagine how your parents felt."

"Oh, the sixties, yes, I knew about all that. Love and freedom. People jumping in and out of bed with each other. But my parents made sure I wasn't—contaminated. I did let my hair grow. And I smoked some grass."

"It might help Bobbi if you told me a little about that time," I said.

"I don't know. I don't like to talk about the past." She turned a little owl-eyed and remote, then went back to her drink.

I remembered Ellen hadn't been in the sixties group photo on Bobbi's bookshelf. For some reason I had assumed Bobbi's affair with Harvey had been on the rebound from Sam, but I didn't really know the chronology. Ellen was the perfect person to fill me in—if I let her get a little drunker.

I might have done it—hell, who am I kidding? I *would* have done just that, but there was the hum of a garage door, then the sound of a door opening and closing somewhere in the house, and Harvey called out: "Ellen?"

Ellen jumped up as he came into the room, her face suffused with gladness, jumped up too quickly with her glass in her hand, swayed, and clutched the sofa arm for support, sloshing liquid on her dress and the flowered upholstery. The dismay on Harvey's face was tinged with disgust, and Ellen's gladness died as swiftly as though he'd thrown a switch.

Harvey grabbed a hand towel off the bar and came over to swab at the spill.

"Sorry," Ellen muttered. "So clumsy—let me—I can do that—"

All she did was dribble more of her drink. Harvey snatched the glass away. "For God's sake, sit down."

But she steadied herself, through sheer force of will, I thought, and said with pathetic dignity, "Delilah needs to talk to you, so I think I'll go, change my clothes, leave you two." She turned to me. "So nice to visit with you, Delilah. Please come back again soon."

She made a reasonably straight-line exit. Harvey slumped down on the sofa with the wet bar rag in his hands and said harshly, "You shouldn't have come here, Delilah. You just gave her an excuse."

"Maybe," I said. "But I don't think she needed one. She was already drinking when I arrived."

"Just the same, you shouldn't be here. I told you not to discuss the case with my wife, and I sure as hell don't conduct business at home."

Harvey's anger was the unreasonable kind that made you want to defend yourself and flare right back. I told myself he wasn't really mad at me. He was mad at circumstance and fate, and I just happened to get in the way. I put down my drink, picked up my handbag, and stood up.

"Got it," I said. "I'll let myself out."

He caught me at the front door, looking chagrined. "Delilah, I'm sorry. I was upset and took it out on you."

"Don't worry about it. I know you have a lot on your mind."

And I had to wonder if part of that burden was guilt, if this crisis was stirring up old feelings for Bobbi.

"I didn't even ask why you wanted to see me," he said.

I told him I really needed the disclosure items, and that I'd like to have the name of the person who overheard Bobbi's and Sandy's argument, and to know if that same person called the police the night Sandy died.

"I'll call first thing tomorrow," he promised. "And what I said before, it was completely uncalled for. I apologize."

"Accepted," I said. "Now can I make a suggestion? Go take care of your wife, Harvey. She needs you."

SO MUCH FOR MY PLANS to get some work done.

I went home, making the mistake of taking the San Diego freeway and getting caught in the crush of weekenders who leave town every Saturday morning and rush home, lemminglike, on Sunday night. I had plenty of time to sit in traffic and pity Ellen Klein in her big, empty house, to think about Harvey and Bobbi and all those old sixties connections.

Which did me a whole hell of a lot of good. The past may prelude, but I sure wasn't hearing the rest of the composition.

Just then three motorcyclists roared past, splitting lanes, weaving in and out of the stalled cars. This made me think of Tony Vero on his hog, and that made me flash on Sam Newley playing golf with his buddy, the Marine colonel, which led me down the street and around the bend and back to Bobbi's almost lethal letter bomb and her conviction that Sandy's death had to do with her work in Newley's office.

This theory was not at the top of my list of possibilities, but I couldn't dismiss it out of hand. Maybe there *was* something dastardly going on in the county; hell, maybe the supervisors had secretly greenlighted a plan to level the Santa Ana Mountains and pave them over.

There was somebody who would know, or, if he didn't know, could certainly find out. Erik Lundstrom. Using Erik as a source of information was not my plan of choice. Anyway, I had a lot of rocks to turn over first. But if it came right down to it, if I came to a dead end, yeah, I'd go ask Erik. I wouldn't like doing it, but I would.

MONDAY MORNING the air was already hot and smelled metallic with ozone when I drove to work, one of those days you hurry from one enclosed, air-conditioned space to another. An inversion layer had shut the damper on L.A., leaving us to stew in our own carbon-burning effluvia.

I arrived at my office with a whole list of things to do: go talk to Bobbi again, call the lab to see if they were able to lift any prints from the bomb-threat envelope, try to nail down some more of Sandy's neighbors for questioning. I would assign Danny the task of checking numbers off Sandy's phone bills.

Meanwhile, I typed up a preliminary report on the insurance fraud case on my old Smith Corona. Once or twice I've actually sat down to the computer keyboard under Danny's tutelage, but on my own I'm sure I would scramble all of Danny's carefully arranged bits and bytes into an electronic omelet.

I was just finishing up when I heard Danny in the outer office.

"Don't shoot, it's just me," he sang out.

"You wear your gas mask today?"

He came to lean against my doorway, a wry grin on his face. "You think you're joking. I actually saw one in a bike shop the other day. I found some more stuff on Sam Newley for you. Oh, and this came." He indicated the manila envelope that he held in his hand along with a file folder. "You expecting something?"

"The coroner's report." I went back to my typewriter and tapped out the last line.

"Maybe that's it," he said. "Funny, though. There's no return address."

I glanced up and saw him turn the envelope to look at it, a nine-by-twelve mailing envelope with my name and address in block letters, big letters, marker-pen black, and some black smudges on the light buff paper—and in a second when time turned to taffy and stretched out forever, I saw Danny stick a finger under the envelope flap and start to rip it open.

I moved a hell of a lot faster than I thought possible, and I yelled Danny's name. The force of my terror made him hesitate as I bounded around the desk, caroming off a sharp corner, and dived for him.

I've been told what happened next. I snatched the envelope from Danny and tossed it into the outer office. Danny thinks I reached for the door to pull it closed.

I don't remember any of that. I doubt I ever will. What I'll never forget is the thunderbolt that struck, the explosion of noise shrieking inside my head, and something big and hard smashing into my back and knocking me into the hole that had suddenly opened up in the middle of the world...

TWELVE

THE NEXT THING I remember was a queer jangling blackness, a lumpy surface beneath me, some kind of weight pressing me down, and, far away, somebody bellowing my name. I remember wishing the guy would shut the hell up and answer the phones, about a million of them all ringing at once. Of course it was Harry, it had to be because Harry wasn't allowed to answer my phone, my million phones, but Danny was, so why wasn't Danny answering—

Danny—

OhgodDanny... Danny with that envelope, peeling open the flap...

I yelled his name. I mean I think I did, who could tell with all that goddamn ringing going on. And I strained to see through neon zigzigs of light. I finally made out a pair of dark eyes inches from mine, then a face. Danny's face. *Two* of him, actually, and both alive. Both mouths moving.

I thought he was saying, "Careful, careful," but I really couldn't tell because Harry was carrying on so. What I did realize was that the lumpy surface beneath me was Danny's wiry body. I lay on top of him in what might have been a lover's embrace except for the slab of wood that lay on top of me.

Then I could make out Harry saying, "Just a minute, hold on," and feel things shifting around and the weight lessening. Harry lifted the wood slab, my God, a *door*, and flung it off with a muted crash.

Harry knelt beside me, his face doubling. Two Dannys were one thing. I wasn't sure about more than one Harry Polk.

Everything did a loop-the-loop as the committee of Dannys and Harrys rolled me over on my back. I got a view of my office. Kind of like the view you get from Colossus up at Six Flags going around that final killer roll. The place looked as though it had been redecorated by Salvador Dali.

Look on the bright side. I was never again going to have to worry about anybody ripping off Danny's computer. Now, if I could figure out what to do with that crater in the outer office floor...

I'VE NEVER BEEN crazy enough, or courageous enough, to surf. I have friends who do. From their descriptions I think my next twenty-four hours were a lot like riding the curl at Steamer's Lane up in Santa Cruz. Up on the bright lip of consciousness, then down into the black depths again.

I registered an ambulance ride, the emergency room. Pain imprinted a lot of this on my memory. Everything hurt: touch, sound, light. So I was more than happy, now and again, to go swooping back into darkness.

A lot of strange faces peered down at me. I thought I saw one familiar one: Erik. The last time I'd been in the hospital—not so long ago, not nearly long enough ago—I had imagined Erik was there. Some kind of mental aberation I get from being bashed by flying furniture and doors.

In my dreams those last few seconds before the explosion played over and over like a video loop. Nothing after the blast. All I saw was that envelope in Danny's hand and his forefinger sliding under the flap. I would bolt out of comforting blackness to scream his name and be reassured that everything was fine, everything was all right.

Later my brain got more cunning. Yeah, you saw his face, my subconscious pointed out. But you didn't see his crushed rib cage or the stump of a leg pumping blood. You didn't see him in an ambulance. You don't see him here in your room, telling you himself he's okay.

At that point my panic must have been obvious because somebody—I'd swear it was Erik—said, "Danny's alive. He's got scrapes and bruises but he's alive. Now, rest, darling, just rest."

Darling?

THIS TIME there was no mistaking that it was Erik sitting beside my bed. He sat in an easy chair, something totally out of place in a hospital room, but there it was and Erik sat in it, his head resting against the high back, his eyes closed. Well, if anybody could have a chair like that brought in, it was Erik Lundstrom.

I was feeling pretty peaceful. Painkillers had given me a nice smooth sea to ride on. The ringing noise still jangled in my head, but muted now, much better. Or was that just the effect of the drugs? I devoutly hoped not. At any rate it was nice to drift along, content with the moment, watching Erik doze.

He looked tired. A shadow of beard along his jaw told me he hadn't been to bed for a while. The stubble was mostly blond with just a little of the premature gray that had turned his hair silver. Instead of aging him, this made him look young and vulnerable. Not that he was so old—forty-nine last May eighteenth, my research revealed. I knew I was mad at him and for good reason, but at that moment I couldn't remember why.

Oh, yeah. He had been involved with old what's-her-name. But he wasn't any more. I confess I had checked that out too.

He opened his eyes. It took a second for the fact that I was awake to register, and then he sat up and said, "Delilah?"

The sound quality was still tinny but definitely improved.

"Anybody see that semi?" I croaked.

He covered my hand with his and reached out with the other one to cup my face. "Christ, you had me scared. Can you hear me all right?"

"Sure," I said dreamily.

I presume he rang for a nurse because one appeared. She looked vaguely familiar with her ruffle of brown curls as she leaned close and said, "Just give us a minute, Mr. Lundstrom." I guess there was a doctor, too. Some guy with rimless glasses and pasty skin poked and prodded and did the old how many fingers and who are you and why are you here routine. He saved the best for last.

"You're a very lucky lady," he said as he shone a penlight into my ears.

"But will I ever play the piano again?"

No sense of humor. He clicked off his little flashlight and said, "We'll have to do some audio tests, of course. It's possible you'll suffer some upper range loss."

"What else?" I asked. "Anything broken?"

"Nothing." He sounded as though he hated to admit it. "You had a minor concussion, lots of bruising. A little like whiplash, only over your whole body. You're going to be pretty stiff and sore."

I didn't appreciate this as the understatement it was until later. Right then I was just happy to be all of a piece, my happiness tempered by the nagging worry about Danny.

"Was anybody else hurt? A young man—Danny Thu—"

"Mr. Thu was treated and released," the nurse said.

The doctor advised me to get some rest and left. The nurse adjusted the IV that flowed into my left hand and announced she was giving me something for pain. "I'm injecting it directly into the IV, you may feel some stinging in your hand."

I did, a majorly strange sensation, but worth it. I got an immediate buzz. When she ushered Erik back in, I could hear their voices over by the door but couldn't distinguish words. At this rate, eavesdropping was definitely going to be a problem.

Erik came over and sat down in the easy chair. Things were starting to haze over again. Great stuff, whatever they were giving me. The fact had sunk in, however, that I must be in a private room and the reason the nurse looked familiar was because she was a private nurse.

"You're doing fine," Erik told me. "You're going to be all right."

"You paying for this again?" I had never received a bill for that other hospital stay. Since medical facilities do not willingly offer charity, I was sure Erik had provided the cash.

"Never mind. Go to sleep, doctor's orders. You want anything first?"

"Just the son of a bitch who blew up my office," I said before I conked out.

WHEN I WOKE UP AGAIN, it was definitely morning. I knew a chunk of time had passed, but not how much, day and nightwise. I tried to turn my head and

got my first taste of what the doctor meant by "a little stiff and sore."

My neck felt as though somebody had removed the
tendons while I slept and replaced them with steel
straps, and then clamped my whole body in a vise.
The pain was somewhat along the lines of pounding
a sore tooth with a hammer. At least the ringing in
my ears had subsided a little more.

I rolled my eyes over far enough to see that Erik
was gone. So was the easy chair.

There was no way I could reach the call button. I
couldn't even *see* the damn thing. If anybody walked
in with another of those nine-by-twelve envelopes, I
was a sitting duck. I had to lie there until the nurse
stuck her curly brown head in.

"Well, good morning," she said.

"Which morning?"

"Wednesday,"

So I had lost a whole day.

"Where is everybody?" I demanded. "If you
don't want a nice big bomb crater in the middle of
your hospital—"

"No problem," she said. "Mr. Lundstrom has an
armed guard right outside your door. I'm Jillian, by
the way." She was a square, no-nonsense woman
with a pleasant face and probably lots of practice
dealing with surly patients. "Now then, ready for
breakfast?"

I was ready for another intravenous pop, but that
wasn't on the menu because she was disconnecting

the IV. Given the choice I preferred being alive and in pain to other alternatives. I agreed to eat if she'd send the guard in first.

I knew the man. His name was Darrel Hayes.

"Hey, Delilah," he said. "Don't you worry. We're taking good care of you. No civilians in or out and we're screening everything."

Darrel had the build and stamina of a Brahma bull. He worked for Charlie Colfax, and while Charlie and I weren't on the friendliest terms anymore, the Colfax Agency hired only the best.

"You've been keeping the police away too?" I asked.

"You betcha. The doc's say-so." He grinned as though he had enjoyed the spectacle. "You up to seeing them now?"

"Yes, as soon as possible."

"Yo," he said. "You got it."

He resumed his post as Jillian breezed in with a tray of food.

"Here we go," she said cheerfully. "Eat that up and we'll see about getting you a nice bath and some therapy. You'll feel much better."

Sure.

Besides bruises, the sponge bath revealed assorted stitches in my calves and just above my left elbow that hurt a lot more after I knew they were there. The physical therapy session left me feeling as though I'd been run over by a freight train. A big fat Tylenol with codeine didn't even take the edge off. Finally, when they finished torturing me, Jillian took me back to my room, where Lieutenant Brady was waiting. He was wearing gray gabardine again. Did the man only own one suit?

He pulled up a chair and watched as Jillian helped me into bed. I gritted my teeth, determined not to moan.

"You don't look too bad," he observed. "Considering."

"Any leads yet?" I hurt too much for small talk.

"Nothing solid. We know it was a letter bomb, loaded with plastic explosives—"

"Delivered in a nine-by-twelve envelope, triggered with a firing pin under spring tension. Come on, Brady. You've seen the threat sent to Bobbi or I'd be talking to another investigator."

"Yeah," he growled. "What I want to know is why I didn't see the thing *before* your office got blown up."

"I wanted Bobbi to turn this over to the police, but she wouldn't listen. Anyway, nobody thought it had anything to do with Sandy's murder."

Well, I had thought about it, but I hadn't really believed it until now.

"Been nice if you'd let me decide what's important to the investigation and what isn't," Brady said. "Not that I think there's any connection. Sandy Renkowski was stabbed."

"Then why are you here?"

"Because I have to wonder what else you're keeping a secret, Mrs. West."

"Dammit, Brady," I said. "Stop waltzing around here. Are you investigating the bombing or not?"

"Oh, I'm on the case." He gave me a smirk, his face strangely naked without his walrus moustache. "I volunteered. You got a suspect for me?"

"I have two. Bobbi told Supervisor Newley, and I'm sure Newley passed the information along to his assistant, Tony Vero."

"You're kidding, right? I haven't been waiting around here to see you the entire time. Let's see. Danny Thu knew about the bomb threat. Your friend, Rita. Wayne Loftland. Bobbi's lawyer. The lab you sent the envelope to—they came up with zip by the way. And who else? Oh, yeah, everybody who works for the Slo-Grow group. Plus all their friends and relatives."

"Okay," I said wearily. "You made your point."

Arguing with him had made my head feel as though somebody were slowly peeling off my scalp, and my ears were ringing again.

"I'm not an unreasonable man," Brady said. "And I don't like coincidence. Give me a logical scenario here."

I closed my eyes and marshaled my flagging strength. "Bobbi and Sandy were close to finding out something, probably involving Newley. Sandy was framed for the park fund theft as a warning to Bobbi, with the bomb threat thrown in for added muscle. But Bobbi's hardheaded and Sandy *does* know something, maybe something going on in Newley's office she doesn't even realize is important yet. So she dies." So it wasn't perfect logic. It was the best I could do at the moment. I gave it one more shot, adding, "Why the knife rather than a bomb? I don't know, maybe the killing was done on the spur of the moment. Bobbi getting the blame is just a little bonus. Everything's looking good. Then I stick my nose in, and boom!"

"Not bad. Maybe you could sell it to Hollywood."

"But you're not buying?"

"'Fraid not. What I think—the bomb thing is just what it seems: a coincidence. They happen. And I already know who killed Sandy."

"Come on, Brady. You have an argument between Sandy and Bobbi. You don't have a motive."

"No? How about Ms. Calder liked the young woman and took her in. Sandy paid her back by going to work for the enemy. Then, to top it off, she turned into a common thief. I know people like Roberta Calder. I started out as a patrolman. I was the one who dragged her and her friends off and threw them in the paddy wagons. These sixties types believe something, they go all the way. I can see Ms. Calder starting an argument with Sandy, tempers run high, and things get out of hand."

My logic might be faulty. His totally sucked.

"You really believe that?" I asked.

"It happens."

At that point Jillian came in and put an end to the interview. I was just as glad. I was too exhausted to debate with Brady, and, anyway, I know how a cop's mind works. Never mind a niggling little detail like motivation; Brady had a clean bust here. Why clutter it up with all these complications?

As Brady headed for the door, I said, "Just one more thing. My gun—I want it back."

"I'll try, but red tape being what it is—" he shrugged, gave me a good-bye salute, and left.

I requested a pain pill and lay there with my eyes closed while the nurse did all her routine checks and updated my chart.

"Jillian?" I said. "Did Mr. Lundstrom say when he'd be back?"

"No. He said to call if you asked for him or needed anything. Should I—"

"No, no," I said quickly. "Just wondering."

Thoughts of Erik and everybody else faded as the codeine finally kicked in and I drifted out on my calm narcotic sea. I was almost asleep when a cold little wind of dread ruffled the waters. As Brady had pointed out, a lot of people knew Bobbi had turned over the bomb threat to me. If the bomber thought I had a lead to his identity, he might also start worrying that I'd told some of those other folks my suspicions.

I might have round-the-clock bodyguards, courtesy of Erik Lundstrom, but nobody else did.

THIRTEEN

SOMETIME WHILE I SLEPT Jillian was replaced by Madge, who was a little older and stouter, definitely Germanic, with a blade of a face, blond hair, and biceps almost the size of Darrel's. She shook me awake around one o'clock and slapped some bland chicken and rice in front of me.

"Eat," she said. "You need your strength."

Well, she was right about that. I was still groggy, so my coordination was off, but I plowed steadily through the food. Stuck in the hospital, there was little I could do for the people who might be next on the bomber's list. I could warn them, but until I got out of here and found the creep, they would be in danger.

After lunch, a fruit basket arrived from the Kleins, containing enough bananas, grapes, and kiwi to feed my private nurses and the guards for a week. Then I was allowed visitors, each scrutinized by the guard. Rita came first, with a big bouquet of flowers, saying she was getting damn tired of visiting me in the hospital and trying very hard not to get mushy. When I warned her about the bomber, she said Farley was already taking precautions and clucking like an old hen.

Danny was next, limping a little. Bruises purpled one side of his face from jaw all the way up beneath his smooth black hair, but he was in one piece. I don't think I believed it until I saw him myself.

"Talk about baptism under fire," I said. "Are you sure you're all right?"

"Yes, thanks to you. You saved my life, Delilah."

"No, I just about got you killed. I like you, Danny. I don't know how I'll ever replace you, but—"

"Stop," he said. "Hold it right there. I'm not quitting and you can't fire me. I know you're going after the guy who sent the bomb, and I'm going to help you. I get really pissed off at people who interfere with my biking."

"Danny—"

"I'm being careful. Believe me. So is my family. We survived Saigon; we can manage this too. Now just tell me what needs to be done while you're here."

What can you do with a kid like that?

If memory served, a lot of my office papers were now so much confetti. I wanted Wayne Loftland to take a look at the place first. As soon as he had, and as soon as the police gave the go-ahead, I told Danny to collect whatever was left and sort it out, to salvage what furniture he could, and to see if he could talk the building manager into giving us an office, anything would do, to put the stuff in.

"Right," Danny said. "You get better. I'll take care of everything."

"Danny, how did you get here?" I knew he didn't have a car.

"The bus."

"Use my van. If my purse didn't survive, there are spare keys in my house. Rita knows. She can let you in. And send in Nurse Rachitt on your way out," I added.

My headache was back and I was beginning to feel like one of those big old clocks somebody forgot to wind. When Madge clomped in, I asked nicely for another painkiller, a telephone, pen and paper. She smirked, closed the blinds, and said, "Later."

"Even when they throw you in jail you get a phone call."

"Hah," she said, handing me my pill.

"Well, you can make this one for me. Call Mr. Lundstrom and tell him I need to talk to him."

It was pretty dark in the room, but I think she nodded agreement. I think she also gave me a knowing grin.

WHEN I WOKE UP in the dim room with my brain still fuzzy from the pain pill, I saw a man sitting beside the bed and naturally said, "Erik?"

"No, it's Matt."

"Oh," I muttered, feeling like a fool. "Dark in here."

"Not that dark."

He was right. There was no denying the observation. Matt with his dark brown hair worn curling below his ears and his mild gray eyes looked nothing at all like Erik.

"Sorry," I said. "Guess I wasn't expecting you."

He must have come from the office, because he was wearing a suit. His shirt collar was unbuttoned, however, and his tie missing. Matt hates ties. In the past year and a half, I've come to know most of his likes and dislikes. He has a weakness for small dogs and children. He will never walk past a panhandler without handing over some money. A comfortable man. Maybe that's all I'd ever had with him—comfort.

"How are you feeling?" he asked.

"Like the Jolly Green Giant used me for batting practice. Could be a lot worse."

We sounded like a couple of polite strangers.

"I was here yesterday," he said. "And Monday. Lundstrom wouldn't let anybody near you. Come to think of it, he's been there between us all along, hasn't he?"

"Matt, I'm sorry."

"Yeah, me too. And I wish things could change, but I don't think they ever will. It's time I face up to that fact." He reached over and brushed my cheek with his fingertips. "Take better care of yourself, Delilah."

Then he stood up and walked away.

"Matt?"

He stopped at the door.

"Matt, I hope you're not sorry. I'm not. We had some good times, didn't we?"

"Yeah," he said. "Just not good enough, I guess. Good-bye, Delilah."

Hell.

Knowing the breakup had been inevitable didn't keep me from feeling sad. Staring at the closed door, I thought of Bobbi's remark: *Old lovers make the best friends.* Maybe. Someday. As far as a relationship with Erik was concerned—snowballs in hell came to mind, especially after the conversation I was planning.

So where did that leave me?

Alone.

Before I could get too morose, Madge came in to take my vitals and assist me to the bathroom—no crutches or wheelchairs necessary, just Madge's muscular arm clamped around my waist. Then she brought me a telephone and actually left me alone to use it. I talked to Wayne but missed Harvey. Then I called Bobbi, who sounded subdued and shaken.

"I blame myself," she said. "If I had listened to you—"

"What's done is done," I said. "Get me a list, Bobbi. Anybody who knew I was working on the bomb threat."

"All right...Delilah? Sam knew. I told him."

"I know."

"It's connected to Sandy's murder, Delilah. It has to be."

I thought so too, and never mind the discrepancy in the M.O., but I said, "Maybe. I promise you I'll find out."

Just after we hung up, my dinner arrived. As I chewed my way through some plain beef and mashed potatoes, Jorge came in, bearing an armful of Consuelo's roses, deep red and richly perfumed, and a card signed by everybody at Mom's.

He surveyed my dinner with disgust. "How they expect you to get well with food like that?"

"Reverse psychology," I said. "Makes you want to get out of here as soon as possible."

After dinner the doctor came back, pronounced me much better, and said he'd set up the audio evaluation for the next morning. He quibbled on how soon I could go home, but finally said that Monday was an outside possibility.

Monday for sure, I promised myself.

Visiting hours ended and still no Erik. I was absurdly disappointed. Brunhilde took away my telephone, put a big heating pad under my shoulders and neck, and said, grudgingly, that she could probably find me some apple juice if I wanted it.

What I really wanted was a very large glass of brandy, but you take what you can get. As she was going out, Erik came in. She gave him a big, smarmy smile and said nothing about visiting hours.

Not that I blamed her. Erik wore a silk suit in a soft slate blue, the color intensifying the blue of his eyes. I didn't know who tailored his clothes, but I knew the man couldn't be paid what he was worth.

"Sorry I got here so late. I had a dinner meeting and just got your message." Erik pulled up a chair and sat beside me, studied me closely. "You look better." A smile crinkled the corners of his eyes. "Pretty good in fact."

A wave of warmth sloshed up my insides. Damn Madge had turned the heating pad up too high.

"I'm sorry if I dragged you away from your meeting," I said.

"You didn't. I wanted to come by anyway. I just wasn't sure of my reception," he said wryly, "now that you're wide awake."

"I really am grateful, Erik."

I've learned to read his face and body language, I suppose, just as he has mine, so I saw the tension and the sudden wariness.

"I mean it," I hurried on. "I know what you've done for me—not just this—everything." He may have started out doing me favors out of guilt, but the payback had gotten way out of hand. I owed him, and I don't like owing people. I hated what I was about to say but I said it anyway. "Can I ask you for one more thing?"

"You know you can. What is it?"

I had a sudden, vivid memory of his hand cupping my face the night before and wanted to say *bring in that easy chair and stay here with me*.

Instead I said, "Information. I need to know if there's anything going on with the County Board of Supervisors, Sam Newley in particular. Something sneaky. Something with a lot of development dollars at stake."

"That's the reason you asked me to come?"

"Well, you're the perfect person to ask," I said lamely, feeling even worse when he moved back in the chair, putting a cool, tangible distance between us.

"There are always development projects in various stages of planning in the county," he said. "Most of them involve plenty of maneuvering, but I've heard of nothing particularly underhanded going on. That doesn't mean there isn't something. Just that I don't know about it."

I could have stopped then. God knows I wanted to, but I didn't—even though I knew I might be risking the chance for a relationship with this man by virtually asking him to spy on his friends. "If you do hear about something, will you let me know?"

"You mean ask around?"

"*No*. I mean *listen*, that's all. This could be dangerous. If anything happened to you—well, I've got enough people to worry about. You have to promise me you won't take any chances. I mean it, Erik."

"I could ask you for the same thing. Of course, I realize I'd be wasting my breath." He stood up. "I'd better go. You need your rest."

"Promise."

"Okay, I'll be careful."

"Good. And you'll give me a call if you hear anything?"

"A call. Right."

He went out and closed the door gently behind him.

Hell.

I LEFT THE HOSPITAL on Monday. I didn't tell Rita for fear she'd insist on coming for me and driving me straight home. I had Danny pick me up in the van.

If my insurance company had been footing the bill, I'm sure they would have shipped me out a lot sooner and let me struggle with outpatient physical therapy. I was tempted to insist on it anyway. However, the quickest way to get better was to swallow my pride and take advantage of Erik's generosity. I wasn't proud of it, but that's what I did.

After a couple of terrible sessions, I actually began to look forward to therapy and improved rapidly. As predicted, the audio tests showed some hearing loss at the high end of the register. This was going to rule out listening for dog whistles and being too critical about stereo components, but I could live with that. The doctor assured me the ringing I was still experiencing would go away in time.

I managed to get a little work done. Bobbi brought in her lists, which included everybody who knew Sandy, those who knew about the bomb threat, and—this one supplied grudgingly—the people she had battled publicly and privately over the environment (Erik Lundstrom among them, along with all the big developers in the county). We went over these last two lists. There wasn't a single person on either that Bobbi would consider a suspect.

Of the office papers Danny rescued, he managed to organize the recent files. The rest I would have to sort myself. He brought a couple of big cardboard boxes into the hospital to get me started. Between that and phone calls, plus the business of getting well, I'd had a busy five days.

Now, as Danny pulled the van into the parking area in back of my building, I could see the boarded-up window marking my office suite. There was no space to put the van, so Danny dropped me by the back door where Harry hovered anxiously. Harry looked older and grayer. He had liver-colored bags under his eyes and a half-dozen bits of tissue stuck to his face to staunch the bleeding from razor cuts.

"Miz West! You ought not to be here your first day—you sure you're okay?"

"Fine, Harry."

And on the whole, I was. Still a little stiff, but I no longer looked like the Nutcracker coming to life in time to "The March of the Toy Soldiers."

"You ain't gonna tackle them steps?" Harry cried with alarm as I headed for the stairs. "You better wait for Danny so's we can help you."

"Just let me lean on you, and I'll be perfectly all right."

"Well—if you're sure."

He offered me his scrawny shoulder and guided me up with a running advisory on where to put each footfall.

At the top, I said, "Thanks, Harry. And thanks for helping Danny. He told me how you kept an eye on things until the two of you got my stuff moved."

"Least I could do," he said. "Shouldna let it happen in the first place."

"Harry, I told you, it's not your fault."

I had talked to Harry on the phone and assured him he was not to blame for what happened, but I could see he was still brooding about it.

"You had no way of knowing what was in that envelope," I said. "But you do know now, and I'm trusting you to keep your eyes peeled. Okay?"

"You bet," he said with some of his old vigor. "Nobody's gonna slip a thing like that past me twice."

Danny arrived then, running lightly up the stairs, carrying my portable car phone. He dug out the key for our temporary office, and turned right toward it. "Pacific Bell is coming after two o'clock. We're going to be a little crowded, but—"

I turned left. I saw the two of them exchange a worried look as they trailed beside me down to my old office suite. The front door was still intact except for the frosted glass window, which had been replaced by boards.

"Just give me a minute," I said.

I took a deep breath, went inside alone, and closed the door behind me.

After Wayne's visit on Friday, Danny had salvaged what he could and disposed of the rest. So there was none of the Daliesque havoc I'd glimpsed after the blast. The room was lit only by shafts of light that arrowed in through cracks in the window boards, but there was plenty of illumination to see where the explosion had gouged out the carpet and subflooring, down to the structural beams. In addition to the hole, flying shrapnel had pockmarked walls and ceilings, and shards of plastic, glass, and metal littered the floor. I was reminded of Wayne telling me about big rocks turned into little-bitty rocks flying around at 27,500 feet per second.

The doorway to my inner office where Danny had stood was considerably larger now, the framework reduced to splinters. I knew where the door had gone.

When Wayne called me at the hospital with his report, he had sounded shaken. From the brisance—which he explained as the shattering effect of the blast—he estimated that my little missive contained one and one-half ounces of plastic explosives. If the bomb had gone off in Danny's hands, both Danny and I would be dead. My slam dunk into the outer office would have bought us distance, but only enough so that our injuries would allow us to die a little more slowly and horribly—except for the door.

Danny remembers that I grabbed the knob and pulled just as the bomb went off. Wayne agrees with that. I'll never know for sure. But we all know that the door was blown off its hinges and that it slammed down on Danny and me, acting like a shield.

Standing there, I felt the chill hand of death touch the back of my neck. I shivered and turned away. Went outside and firmly closed the outer door behind me.

"Okay," I said to Danny. "Let's get to work."

FOURTEEN

MY NEW OFFICE was crowded, all right. Not because Danny had managed to salvage so much, but because the place was only slightly larger than a broom closet. "It was take it or leave it," Danny said. The building manager was, understandably, not thrilled to have a tenant who received letter bombs.

I surveyed what remained of the furniture with dismay. My steel desk looked as though somebody had worked it over with a hammer. One heavy metal leg was bent enough so that Harry had to put a board under it to keep the desk from listing to starboard. The file cabinet that once stood in my outer office was now in small pieces embedded in the carpet over there. The other sat here in the corner, a huge dent in the side, so out of square it was a major effort to open and close a drawer.

Good-bye computer, printer, and typewriter. Adios, Mr. Coffee. An ancient typewriter table that had held the coffee machine survived. Danny now used it for his old electric portable, unearthed from a closet at home and brought in to tide us over. A couple of chairs and we were in business—sort of.

As we began cataloging what was left of the current files, I found myself thinking wistfully of Madge and my afternoon nap. "I think there's enough here to reconstruct the fraud report," I said. "How about I write it up tonight in longhand and you type it tomorrow?"

"Okay." Danny opened another folder. "You remember Mr. Tilson's old girlfriend? Well, I followed up on your suggestion. Her husband was in the service, all right. He died at Midway, 1942. Now what?"

"Remarriage? Or you might find some of the husband's relatives."

That took care of everything except for Bobbi Calder's case. Very little of Danny's original research on Sam Newley and Tony Vero survived, but he'd gathered most of the information again. We had the rosters from Bobbi. Despite Bobbi's conviction that none of these people could possibly be connected to either the murder or the bombing, and despite the fact that lots of names appeared on more than one list, there was still a daunting number of people to check out.

My purse had been tucked into the bottom drawer of my desk, so it had survived, along with the inventory of Sandy's phone calls for the past six months. In addition, in a brown manila envelope grimly reminiscent of the one containing the letter bomb, was the autopsy report from the coroner's office, which had arrived this morning.

"Welcome to the glamorous world of the private investigator," I said to Danny as I opened the file on Sam Newley.

The folder was even fatter than the original, mostly with news clippings. Skimming them, it seemed our boy Newley was well heeled, well connected, and, if you believed his PR, well liked in the county. I lingered on the clipping of Sam and his buddy, Colonel George Raeford. I had not forgotten that Wayne had put the military at the top of the supply chain for plastic explosives. Of course, I didn't believe that a full bird colonel had personally handed Sam Newley enough C-4 to blow my office sky high, but as Jack used to say, there's more than one way to slip the fur off an unsuspecting feline.

"What?" Danny looked over at the clipping. "Should I put together a file on Colonel Raeford?"

"No. I think this requires some personal attention."

Tony Vero's file was next. A homeboy, born Santa Ana, California, 1959, Santa Ana H.S., business degree Cal State Fullerton. No military service. He'd gone to work for Newley Development, Inc., straight out of college. Went from there to his job as Newley's assistant four years ago. His DMV record was clean, except for two speeding tickets in the past three years, and it showed registrations for Vero's BMW and his Harley motorcycle.

"Yuppie biker," I said, remembering Vero on his hog.

Danny grinned. "Keep reading."

The next thing in the file was a printout of a Sheriff's Department rap sheet for Anthony Dominic Vero. I didn't want to ask how Danny obtained it. Vero's record showed an arrest in June, 1977, disturbing the peace and use of a controlled substance, which translated into a party bust and some marijuana joints. After that he was Mr. Straight Arrow until two years ago, when he was arrested on drunk and disorderly and aggravated assault charges in a brawl at Cook's Corner, a biker's hangout in what used to be the county backcountry near Silverado. The charges had been dropped. Maybe the charges against everybody in the fight had been dismissed. Maybe working for a County Supervisor made no difference whatsoever.

Sure.

"Seems old Tony runs with a rougher crowd than I thought," I said. "Wonder who some of them are. Anything in the papers about the incident?"

"Just a mention in both the *Times* and the *Register*," Danny said. "No names."

"Try the local paper down there." I wished I'd known if Vero had a juvenile record. Even if he did, it would be sealed, and records that went that far back wouldn't be computerized. "Now, this other stuff—"

I looked at the assorted lists and kneaded the muscles in the back of my neck, which were stiffening up and starting a headache. Since I wasn't going to let Danny anywhere near anybody with the slightest potential of being our bomber, I gave him the record of Sandy's telephone calls and told him to start working backward.

On cue, the Pacific Bell installer arrived.

This time three really did make a crowd. I asked Harry to stick around with the installer and lock up afterward, gathered up the files, and had Danny take me home.

AFTER SOME MOTRIN and half an hour on the couch with my eyes closed, I was ready to check in with my answering service. Rita herself came on the line.

"I hope you're talking to me from a horizontal position," she said sternly. "And don't lie about going to work today. I went by your office and forced Harry to admit it."

"I confess," I said. "If it makes you feel any better, I didn't enjoy it. Unfortunately, I have bills to pay. So I'd better have my messages."

Not a lot of calls, since most people knew I was in the hospital. Nothing from Erik. Mostly my calls were from worried clients. During the next hour I managed to reassure the ones with work in progress. I got a unanimous *sorry, but we're hiring somebody else* from the prospective clients. Nobody wanted to put their corporate work into the hands of a bomb target.

All the more reason to find the bomber as soon as possible. I brewed a pot of strong coffee, picked a business card from my shoebox collection, and called the El Toro Marine base. When the base operator put me through to press relations, I said that I was Camille Dwyer of the *Los Angeles Times*—the name on the business card—and that I wanted to do an article on the Marines, a positive piece emphasizing all the things the Corps contributed to Orange County. Maybe good PR was in short supply for the military just then, because they readily agreed to give me a tour and to set up an interview with Colonel Raeford for the following morning at eleven hundred hours.

I might have attempted to go looking for some of the people on Bobbi's lists, but I was grounded. Danny had driven the van down to Mission Viejo to visit the *Saddleback Valley News* office. While I rummaged in the freezer for something to microwave for dinner, Ellen Klein called.

"How are you?" she asked anxiously. "Did you get the fruit I sent to the hospital?"

"Yes, it was very nice, thank you."

I truly felt sorry for the woman, but I wasn't up to dealing with her, and I certainly didn't want to have another argument with Harvey. Still, what could I do short of hanging up?

"I'm sorry about the other night," she said. "I feel like such an idiot. I had a little problem with alcohol at one time, and now if I have just one drink, Harvey overreacts."

I might have pointed out that she'd had a lot more than one drink, and that I wouldn't be surprised if she had a tumbler full of straight vodka in her hand right now, but instead I said politely, "Don't worry about it. I understand."

"Well, I know it must have been awkward for you. I planned to call and apologize, then I heard about what happened to you, and I felt just terrible."

I thanked her for her concern, mentioned my fatigue—which God knows was real enough—and finally got her off the line. I immediately dialed Harvey's office. He was still there, although it was past six o'clock.

"I wanted to tell you your wife called," I said. "So there's no misunderstanding, it was a short conversation, and nothing was said about the case."

"Was she drinking?"

"I don't know."

"I'm sorry you got mixed up in this," he said. "I've asked her not to call you. I don't know why she keeps doing it."

"It's all right, Harvey, really. I just wanted you to know." Happy to change the subject, I said: "What about the discovery items? Do you have them from the D.A. yet?"

He had them and promised to messenger Sandy's address book and current phone record to my temporary office tomorrow along with information about the witness. The woman, Valerie Ryan, lived directly below Sandy. As I suspected, she had also called the police on the night of Sandy's murder after hearing a scream—Bobbi's scream when she found Sandy's body, a good twenty minutes before I arrived. This gave testimony to the speedy police service.

"According to her statement, that was all she heard," Harvey said. "And she saw nobody going in or out."

"Too bad," I said. "I still want to talk to her."

"So do I, but I'm afraid we'll have to wait. She's out of town until the weekend."

I promised I'd let him know if I turned up anything and hung up just as Danny came back wearing a triumphant grin and bearing a pizza, thus saving me from another prepackaged meal. First things first. We finished off our deep-dish, double cheese and pepperoni dinner, and then Danny produced a copy of an article that had run in the *News* about the biker brawl at Cook's Corner two years before.

There was no mention of Tony Vero, but there were several other names. Computer fodder, Danny said, which he would process right away.

"Do you think any of these guys will turn out to be important?" he asked.

"Probably not. But all we can do is track down every lead and hope something comes up we can use."

By then I was more than happy to say goodnight to Danny and send him on home. Assorted aches and pains reminded me I was just home from the hospi-

tal and ought to be considering my doctor's advice
about taking it easy. Therefore, I poured myself a
large brandy, took my drink into the living room,
and sat on the couch with my feet up while I wrote
the insurance fraud report. That done, I opened the
envelope from the coroner's office, paused long
enough to drink the rest of my brandy, then took out
the autopsy report.

As Harvey had said a week ago when we talked
about it, no surprises from the preliminary estimate
of time and cause of death. Sandy had no drugs or
alcohol in her bloodstream. Judging from the position and the angle of the first wound, her killer had
been right-handed and taller than Sandy—but then
almost anybody was. The coroner estimated a height
of five-eight to six feet. As I had guessed, the first
stab had been fatal, delivered with enough force to
go in through the rib cage and slice down into the left
ventricle of the heart.

The impersonal words of the report conjured up
Sandy's body, the slashes in the bloody pink blouse,
the torn flesh beneath the fabric, the sticky, darken-
ing stain on the carpet. Remembering, I skimmed the
rest of the report and almost missed the information
included in a mandatory section required by the state
of California on every female cadaver.

Even though there is no suspicion of rape or assault, the sexual organs are examined and the results
reported to the Health Department, these reports
used for medical studies. I wasn't sure how inter-

ested the medical researchers would be in Sandy because her sexual organs showed no abnormalities.
She had been a normal, twenty-seven-year-old
woman with everything in working order.

She had also had sexual intercourse sometime
within five hours before the time she died.

FIFTEEN

NEXT MORNING I did the exercises prescribed by the therapist—not much fun but necessary. Then I showered and dressed in silk slacks and a jacket that covered up my assorted stitches and bruises. To the pale yellow suit I added a white silk blouse, unbuttoned to show a modest amount of unbruised cleavage.

My excursion to the El Toro Marine base might prove to be a tricky expedition. However, in my experience, military establishments are a place where men are men, and women, especially those in clingy clothes, are sex objects, and I was not above taking advantage of that fact.

When Danny arrived to pick me up, I said that I would drive. No sense wasting Danny's time chauffeuring me around. I felt strangely wooden behind the wheel, and by the time we got to the office, I could feel the strain in my neck muscles.

"You sure you'll be all right if I go out?" Danny asked.

"I'm sure." Well, I wouldn't be great, but I would manage.

Danny's bicycle was still in Harry's supply closet, stored there since the day of the bomb blast. Danny only said vaguely that he wanted to use a friend's computer. I had a feeling that I would soon know whatever the police files held on those bikers arrested out at Cook's Corner.

"Try to find some time to work on that list of Sandy's phone calls," I called after him.

Now that I knew I was right about Sandy having a lover, I was determined to find the man. There was a good chance that he was the last person to see Sandy alive. She might even have confided in him whatever it was she had wanted so urgently to tell Bobbi and me just before she died.

Or he might just be a crazy man bent on destruction by whatever means that came to hand, be it a butcher knife or a bomb, with no connection to Sam Newley whatsoever.

So where did that leave me? With a hell of a lot of things that needed checking out—including all those neighbors in Sandy's apartment building. And Valerie Ryan, once she arrived home. If I budgeted my strength, maybe I could get over there later today.

For now I looked at my watch and decided I had time to call Bobbi before going off to the El Toro Marine base.

I told her what I had discovered in the autopsy report.

"Amazing what we don't know about people, isn't it?" she said.

"Are you sure Sandy never mentioned dating anybody? Even casually?"

"No. She was entitled to a private life, of course, but wouldn't you think I would just say: Have you made any new friends, Sandy? Are you dating anybody? Are you having any fun? I guess I was just too damn busy worrying about trees and coyotes and fucking butterflies—" She broke off, then went on harshly, "Nobody's come to me to say he loved her, that he misses her. Then, of course, why should he, considering that I'm charged with her murder. I could ask Harvey. He was her attorney, so he saw more of her than I did those last weeks."

"That would help," I said. "Maybe the two of you could think of a likely candidate."

"All right. Have you come up with anything else?"

I hedged. "One or two leads."

"What are they?"

"It's too early to talk about it, Bobbi. What I do is not an exact science. It's like having a big ball of string. You pick off a piece and follow it. Mostly you get these useless little ten-inch pieces, but, if you keep going, eventually you find the one that unravels the whole thing."

"Well, I hope this process doesn't take too long," she said. "I've already talked to Harvey this morning. The D.A. is going all out to make sure they try me as soon as possible."

I thought of the mountain of work that lay ahead. "I may have to add an extra investigator. Can you handle that? Or maybe you want to go with some-

body else, Bobbi. You'll get no guilt trips from me if
you do. I'll continue to look for the bomber, of
course. I want him for personal reasons now."

"No," she said forcefully. "Forget anything I said
earlier. Get some help if you need it, but, please, stay
on the case. You want this guy almost as much as I
do. Nobody else is going to feel that way."

She said she would send me some more money; we
agreed on an amount, and I promised I'd keep her
informed.

As I hung up, a patrolman arrived with Harry on
his heels. It was Ron Dickey, the cop who had su-
pervised the visit to Sandy's apartment—the legitimate visit—bearing a package for me from
Lieutenant Brady.

"It's okay, Harry," I said. Harry reluctantly retreated, at least as far as the hallway.

"The lieutenant wants you to open this and make
sure everything's okay," Dickey said.

This was a shoebox-sized carton containing my
gun, unloaded, but all six cartridges were there in the
box. Either Brady had cut through the red tape, or
somebody higher up had done it for him.

"Lieutenant wants a signed receipt," Dickey said.

"Glad to." I scrawled my name on the form he
thrust at me. "And thank you for your kind and at-
tentive personal service."

He gave me a look that said he didn't know what
that meant, but he didn't like it anyway. "Yeah," he
said and stomped out.

Silly how much better I felt having the gun in my possession. It would have made no difference last week when the bomber paid a call. He had simply left his padded envelope downstairs propped on top of the letter boxes when Harry wasn't looking. Anyway, most of the time when I needed a weapon the damned thing was never in reach.

Still, I felt unreasonable relief as I loaded the thirty-eight, tucked it into my purse, left the office, and headed for El Toro.

MY LIAISON at the base was Lieutenant Hollis Smeal— "Call me Holly," he said, standing about five inches closer than was necessary and holding my hand about five seconds too long. He was in his early twenties with a hard, muscular body set off by the sharply creased khakis, one of those men who might really prefer beach bunnies but will home in on any female who is handy. His dark hair was short, crisply barbered, and he had the eyes of a stalking tiger.

I saw no glimmer of recognition there. The article in the paper on the bombing had included an old photo of me, but I was vain enough to think the picture was a terrible likeness.

He escorted me personally to the colonel's office, promising a tour of the base as soon as I talked to Raeford. My silk suit was too damn hot, but at least the droplets of sweat rolling down into the V of my blouse weren't wasted. Holly didn't miss a drop.

George Raeford was a different kettle of very old fish. Clingy pants and cleavage were wasted on him. He was a rawboned Ichabod Crane with a golfer's tan, a good ten years older than Sam Newley. Pebble brown eyes didn't smile, but then neither did his thin lips.

He stood up just long enough to say, politely, "Miss Dwyer," then motioned me to a chair on the other side of his big desk and sat back down.

"Thank you for seeing me, Colonel Raeford," I said. "I know how busy you are."

"My pleasure." He reached for a thin, black cigar that smoldered in an ashtray and smelled like old rope soaked in sewage.

I launched into my spiel about doing a puff piece on the base, throwing in my own personal admiration of the Corps, trying for a blend of journalistic sales pitch and feminine charm while he rolled his cigar and watched me with those stone-smooth eyes.

I plowed on doggedly about what a great opportunity this would be to publicize the base's close ties with the community, getting more unnerved by the minute. What qualified him to head up press relations? Certainly not charm and personality. Prying information from this man would take more skill and stamina than I possessed. Better to take my chances with Hollis Smeal.

"I won't take up any more of your time," I said. "I'm looking forward to touring the base. I'll be in touch if I need any more information."

"You do that," he said.

So I was on my way out of there, free and clear, almost to the door when I said, "By the way, Colonel, I believe we have a mutual acquaintance—Sam Newley."

"Oh?" Finally a flicker of interest. "You know Sam Newley?"

"Yes, I did a story on his park fund. I remember seeing a piece in his clip file that mentioned you. Have you known him long?"

"A while," he said. "Nice of you to come out, Miss Dwyer. I'm sure Lieutenant Smeal will take good care of you."

Ah, well, I tried.

Holly waited in the outer office. I gave him a big smile and let him lead me outside to a jeep. As we left the low, nondescript buildings that made up the headquarters' offices and barracks, Holly pointed with pride to the enlisted men's mess, saying it was nothing like the old version of a chow hall.

"More like a food court," he said. "There's a salad bar, a bakery that makes terrific croissants. You can have pasta or even sushi. Of course, the officer's mess is even better. We'll come back and have lunch."

We headed for the air field, each rattle and bounce of the jeep jarring my tender back muscles. The sun beat down fiercely on the sere brown hills and heat shimmered on the long runways. If we'd had some eggs, we could have made lunch right there on the tarmac. Three fighter jets shrieked past, practicing touch-and-go landings in formation. My sore eardrums pulsed in protest.

As we cruised through parked fighters and huge troop carriers, I said, "Know what I'd like to see, Holly? One of those practice demolition things you guys do."

"We don't do much of that here any more," he said. "Mostly they do the demos at Pendleton."

"Oh, gee," I said, "really? Oh, but you must have all kinds of stuff here—missiles and explosives—"

I caught a flash of wariness in his eyes, and I added hastily, "I don't expect you to tell me *what*, Holly. I'm sure it's classified. I'm just thinking that the readers might worry about things like that falling into the wrong hands."

"Like what?"

"I don't know—like dynamite."

He gave me a patronizing smile. "We mostly use plastics now. And it's all strictly accounted for."

"Well, that's a relief," I said.

The jets screamed past again, setting off that unpleasantly familiar ringing in my head. I was more than happy to have Holly leave the air field and race back to headquarters. I would even eat sushi as long as the mess hall was quiet and the raw fish came with iced tea.

Holly parked the jeep and helped me down, his hands lingering on my waist. "I need to check in, then we'll go have lunch."

"Great," I said.

Lunch was not on the menu, however. An M.P. waited for me in Holly's office, huge, black, and unsmiling, with the message that Colonel Raeford wanted a word with me. Poor Holly stood there with his mouth open while the M.P. hustled me away.

We double-timed it over to the colonel's, not my best gait just then. I knew I'd been made even before the M.P. thrust me into Raeford's office. This time Raeford didn't bother with civility, let alone politeness.

"Your identification," he said coldly.

"Gee," I said. "Sorry. I gave my last card to the lieutenant. Always running out—you know how it is."

"Driver's license," Raeford said. "Hand it over."

I gave him what I hoped was a disarming smile. "You got me, Colonel." I handed over my state ticket showing I was a licensed P.I. "I'm investigating a bombing that almost killed two people. The explosive used was C-4, and I want to find out where the bomber got his supply."

"I see." He handed back my I.D. "Why didn't you simply ask me about it?"

"Oh, silly I know, but somehow I had the crazy idea you wouldn't be real straightforward with me. How about it? Any chance that C-4 could've come from your stockpile?"

"No," he snapped. "Absolutely not. This base has strict routines to account for explosives. All military units do."

He proceeded to explain in detail then how many federal laws I'd broken and how tempted he was to slap me in the brig. By the time he was finished, I was more than happy to be merely escorted off the base.

On the way home, it occurred to me that in some countries I would have been shot first and questioned later, some small comfort. Had I raised Raeford's suspicions by mentioning Sam Newley? Chalk it up, I told myself.

How had I explained the theory of detection to Bobbi? A ball of string, short pieces and long pieces. I had left out the part about bumbling around and having people snatch that long piece right out of your hands.

At home I showered and changed my clothes, ate a sandwich, and took some Motrin. I thought about the nap the doctor had advised, a passing thought as I drove back to the office.

Danny was gone, but he must have come back at some point because he had typed the insurance report and left the mail stacked on my desk—no suspicious envelopes, just bills and sales pitches. Rita's service reported no messages. I tried Wayne, but Peggy said he was out.

I gave some thought to another investigator. Charlie Colfax could certainly supply an excellent person. He might even give me a break on the price.

He probably *would* give me a discount and then bill
Erik for the difference. So, no way. I called a couple
of other people in small agencies like mine and finally got a commitment for Friday.

While I waited for Danny, I worked on Bobbi's list
of people who knew about the bomb threat, using
her marginal notes for the culling process.

Walter and Mavis Pierce—In their seventies; she
takes in homeless cats, thirty-two at last count; he
volunteered last year to go paint baby harp seals to
keep them from being slaughtered but since he's in a
wheelchair Greenpeace turned him down.

I thought I could safely put the Pierces at the bottom of the list.

The phone rang. It was Tony Vero. "Mr. Newley
is on the line for you," he said with no preamble.

"Well, Sam," I said. "What a surprise."

"The police were just here." He was coldly furious. "Routine, they said, but I know damn well why
they came. And George Raeford called to tell me
about that little charade of yours out at El Toro this
morning. This is going to stop right now, do you hear
me? I'm filing suit for harassment and slander and
anything else I can come up with. Get yourself a
good lawyer, Mrs. West. You're going to need one."

I winced as he slammed down the phone in my ear.
Well, whatever caused Raeford to tumble to my
identity, he wasted no time passing on the news. I
wondered if I was going to dig myself a hole so big
even Erik couldn't pull me out. I wondered if there

was enough floor space in this office for my sleeping bag. Of course, I could always set up housekeeping in the van. Park on the streets or in my friends' driveways. I've heard there's a whole little community of the homeless living in the one rest area between L.A. and San Diego, switching from southbound to northbound sides of the freeway when the cops hassle them.

Look on the bright side. If Brady had questioned Newley, he hadn't totally discounted my suspicions about the bombing. He might get lucky and actually find something useful. This was not something to count on, however, so I went back to Bobbi's lists.

I had come up with half a dozen outside possibilities when Danny arrived looking enormously pleased with himself. He handed me a printout that could only have come from the Orange County Sheriff's Department files.

"Fifteen arrests at that fight out at Cook's Corner," he said. "Tony Vero was the only one who got away clean."

"Certainly couldn't have been any influence used there." I scanned the printout. "Nice bunch of guys. Hello—" I read: "Zackery Pellissier, staff sergeant, and Sal Thomas Rizzo, corporal, U.S.M.C. Fined and released to custody, base commander, U.S.M.C.A.S., El Toro."

"What do you think?" Danny asked.

"I think I may be bailing your butt out of jail one of these days along with this anonymous hacker friend of yours."

"I'd like to give you more on this Rizzo and Pellissier, but messing with the Fed's computer can be tricky."

"Then don't even try," I said. "You can work on these people instead." I handed him the names from Bobbi's list. "See what you can dig up. By the way, did you get a chance to do any more backtracking on Sandy's phone calls?"

"I'm working on it," he said. "I might be able to finish it up by tomorrow. I could call these names over, but it's better if I'm there with the computer."

"Then go."

He was no sooner out the door when Wayne Loftland returned my call. I told him about my trip out to El Toro and Colonel Raeford's flat statement concerning the military's safeguards on explosives.

Wayne laughed. "Let me tell you about their strict routines. When these guys check out explosives for test firings, they sign for a whole case. Nothing says they have to *use* a whole case, you understand. So they're way off in the mountains when a storm blows in, and say they've used up maybe half the stuff. Are they going to stay up there with lightning zapping around? No, ma'am. So now they got maybe half a case of HE and some ordnance sergeant is going to give them hell about the paperwork when they bring it back. Sometimes these boys come up with real interesting solutions. Like throwing the leftovers into an old quarry on the military reservation, that was a good one I heard about. Now suppose you get some guy who's hurting for money and not too morally righteous. He could set up a damn good sideline business for himself.''

''And that kind of business would bring our dealer into contact with some pretty unsavory types,'' I said.

''You got somebody like that in mind?'' Wayne asked.

''Maybe. Couple of things I'm checking out. I'll let you know.''

''Okay. Meantime, I put out some feelers.''

''Feelers?'' I said. ''You're retired, Wayne.''

''Yeah, well, no big deal. I'm just asking around. There's still a few people who owe me.''

''You don't have to do this,'' I said.

''Yeah, I do. I've lost too many friends already,'' he said soberly. ''I don't want to lose another one.''

''All right, but if you hear anything, call me right away.''

He promised he would, and we chatted a while longer about his kids, about my recovery, about a backyard luau he and Peggy were planning to celebrate their anniversary, and how of course he wanted me to be there.

Along about then would have been a real good time for a hunch or a premonition, but all I had was my neck stiffening up and a hell of a headache come on. So after I hung up, I gathered up the files and headed home, the only things on my mind the relief that I might for once beat the rush-hour traffic and that I might even get over to the Garden View Apartments for some interviews.

SIXTEEN

ONCE I WAS HOME I made the mistake of sitting down on the couch, and that old devil fatigue delivered a sucker punch that left me muttering, "Tomorrow," and closing my eyes.

When I opened them, two hours had passed. Forget work. All I wanted was some food, a soak in the complex's hot tub, and about eight hours in bed.

COME MORNING a physical therapy session gave me so much relief from the stiffness and soreness that I began to feel like a normal person. On the way to work, I made mental schedules and began to think I wasn't going to need another investigator after all. Then I walked into my office and found both the building manager and my insurance adjustor lying in wait.

Dealing with them took most of the morning and still nothing was settled. I thought my policy covered everything short of the sun going nova, but the adjustor wasn't about to commit to any settlement until he'd checked every loophole twice.

In the midst of all this, Danny plugged away on the telephone, and the messenger from Harvey's office arrived with Sandy's address book and the list of her most recent phone calls. By the time I got rid of the adjustor, I was starving, irritated, and desperately in need of some strong coffee. We gathered up Danny's notes and adjourned to Mom's. There we got a corner booth and prompt service.

I ordered a ham on rye, hold the stuffing—everything at Mom's comes with a side of stuffing—and lemon meringue pie for dessert. Danny just wanted soup. My coffee cup got refilled after every two sips.

Danny had found nothing interesting on the people from Bobbi's lists. This did not, however, eliminate the need for some legwork. Computer searches can only reveal so much. Meanwhile he had gone through three months of Sandy's phone bills. Another zero.

Tracking down the two Marines, Rizzo and Pellissier, seemed to me the logical next step. But I also wondered if I shouldn't expand my inquiries. Wayne had mentioned legitimate explosives dealers. That should probably be looked into, and I wasn't sure the police would follow through. At this point I didn't even want to think about terrorist groups as sources.

Ideally, I should also interview people close to both Sam Newley and Tony Vero. Not to mention the interviews left to do at the Garden View Apartments. And we hadn't even started on Sandy's address book.

Jesus, I didn't just need another investigator. I needed a whole army of them.

Like the Colfax Agency.

No. Not yet.

Back at the office, I brought in the car phone and Danny and I both got busy. While he checked out Sandy's recent phone calls, I tried Wayne to see if he'd gotten any nibbles. Nobody home. I left a message on the machine.

I figured everybody out at the El Toro Marine base had been alerted not to cooperate with me, so I came up with some inventive and innovative ways to ask about Rizzo and Pellissier. I still spent two hours finding out that Sergeant Pellissier had been discharged six months ago and that Corporal Rizzo was now stationed at Camp Pendleton. No point in contacting Rizzo by phone. And it was already too late to drive down to Camp Pendleton. I decided I'd be better off leaving it until tomorrow. For now I'd concentrate on Sandy's address book and then, during dinner when they were more likely to be home, her neighbors.

The address book contained dozens of entries, none of which were marked with hearts, flowers, or anything else that might point to somebody who was more than a friend. Just looking at all those phone numbers made my neck muscles tighten up.

After another hour of calls, A through F in Sandy's book, I knew I'd better get started over to Sandy's place. As it was, I'd be in the thick of traffic. Danny had worked his way through Sandy's current telephone record and turned up nothing. He said he'd do some more backtracking before he left.

Outside, an ocean breeze had cooled down the temperature to something close to perfection. Toward the Pacific the sky was already hazy with high streamers of fog. I gave silent thanks for the marine layer moving in to moderate the heat, opened the van windows, and enjoyed the air.

Although I wasn't really hungry, I stopped at Burger King. I'd made it through the day without any Motrin, but now I needed some to get me through the evening, and I couldn't take the medication on an empty stomach.

I still arrived at Sandy's apartment building by six-thirty. While the dinner hour may be perfect for finding people at home, they are also tired, hungry, and hostile. Most of them said they hadn't seen or heard anything. Some had vague recollections that only added contradictions and confusion. Three people flatly refused to talk to me, although one agreed, grudgingly, to let me call him for an appointment. Nobody invited me in, so I was on my feet the whole time.

By eight-fifteen I'd canvassed all the apartments, upstairs and down, on Sandy's side of the U. I even knocked on Valerie Ryan's door and got no answer. Enough. I went home.

The drive was done on auto pilot, and to tell the truth I didn't even think about checking my service until I was heading for what was fast becoming my roosting spot on the couch. Remembering, I sighed, detoured to pick up the portable phone, and dialed.

I had received only two calls, both from Wayne
Loftland. He'd called at five-thirty and left a message that he needed to speak to me right away. Then
he called again at six and this time he said to tell me
that he couldn't wait, that he'd gone to meet some
people at Newport Pier and would be in touch as
soon as he got back.

It had never occurred to me to give Wayne my car
phone number, and I'd had too many other things on
my mind to think about checking in with the service
earlier. Filled with apprehension, I dialed the Loftland house.

Peggy picked up the phone on the first ring.

"It's Delilah," I said. "Is Wayne there?"

"No, he's not. I went to pick up the boys from
baseball practice, and when we got home Wayne was
gone. He left me a note, said not to wait dinner, that
he'd be back soon. But he hasn't called, Delilah, and
I'm getting a little worried. Do you know what this
is about?"

"I think so," I said. "Did he say anything else in
his note?"

"No."

"Was he driving the pickup?"

"Yes—what is it? Is he in some kind of trouble?"
Wayne might be retired, but Peggy still had the anx-
ieties of a cop's wife.

"I doubt it, Peggy. But I'm going to make sure.
Give me an hour. If you don't hear from me, call the

Newport police. Tell them to come down to the
Newport Pier and check on us."

"Now I *am* worried," she said with growing
alarm.

"It's probably nothing." I didn't believe that for
a minute, but there was no sense in scaring her more
than she already was. "Wayne probably ran into
some old buddies and they're having a beer. I'll call
you."

I took two minutes to exchange my skirt for jeans
and my sandals for running shoes, then grabbed a
sweatshirt and bolted for the van. On the drive to
Newport, I told myself Wayne knew what he was
doing. He'd arranged his meet in a place where there
were sure to be plenty of people around. It was summer, after all, when the Balboa peninsula is wall to
wall with tourists and sun-lovers.

But the sun had long since gone when I rolled
across the bridge that spans PCH and the tail end of
the Lido channel, and traffic was light. Fog drifted
in a fine gray mist. Sensible tourists were out to late
dinners or over at Disneyland lining up for the elec-
trical parade and the nightly fireworks. As I approached the turnoff to the pier, the streets grew even
more deserted.

The peninsula is like a great big sandspit, harbor
on one side, the Pacific on the other, the ocean side
rimmed with beaches. Balboa Boulevard runs right
down the middle.

I turned off Balboa onto McFadden. After a short block, the street widened to accommodate a couple of rows of parking, then ended right at the pier entrance in a broad sweep of concrete decorated with some palm trees. The fog was so thick I could just barely see the pavilion-styled city building that houses the beach patrol and emergency services, and sits off to the left of the ramp that leads up to the pier. I wondered if the restaurant and bar out at the end of the pier closed down on nights like this.

I sat in the van, engine idling, trying to decide where to start looking for Wayne. To my left a handful of cars and a couple of motorcycles nosed in to the on-street parking meters, there, I supposed, for Charlie's Chili, which was the only thing open in the short strip of businesses.

Dead ahead two large public rest rooms stood on either side of the concrete pier entrance, testimony to the number of people who flock here during the day. Just to the right was a handful of fishing shacks, dark now, but I know what they look like: a kind of mini-mall of them built in Knotts Berry Farm rustic with some yellow-slickered plaster fisherman and plaster gulls decorating the rooftops. The small dory fleet that uses the shacks is real enough and so was the fishy odor wafting my way. During the day, the dorymen provided freshly caught bonita and snapper and sea trout for the locals and color for the tourists.

Ocean Boulevard went off to the right for a few short blocks. On the land side of Ocean a strip of small shops cater to the T-shirt, postcard, and walk-away food trade—all closed now. Through the mist I could see a few lights—Blackie's Bar, probably, and the handful of rentals down the way. A parking lot ran along the other side of the street next to the beach. In the dim yellow glow of a streetlamp, I saw a lone vehicle parked in the lot about half the distance of one of those short blocks away. A pickup—I was sure it was, the thought prompting a sour knot of dread to form in my stomach.

The parking lot's only one aisle wide, one way, and you're supposed to go down to the far end to enter. I went in the wrong way and swung around to park beside the truck—Wayne's old blue Toyota with the dent in the left front quarter panel.

Fog had condensed on the pickup, turning the wet windows opaque. I shut off my engine, slipped the thirty-eight from my purse, and climbed out. The night air was chill and damp, heavy with the smell of brine. Waves boomed on the beach out in the foggy darkness.

Fear dried my throat as I went to the truck and reached for the door handle. Unlocked. I opened the door. The cab was empty. The dome light showed nothing more sinister than a crumpled candy wrapper on the floor.

I chuffed out a sigh of relief and looked around. Over the sound of surf, I could hear a distant beat of drums and guitars. I couldn't tell where the music was coming from. Not from Blackie's, however. No cars out front, so it was probably closed.

Okay, so I'd try Charlie's Chili. Wayne was probably over there working on a Bud Light just as I had predicted to Peggy.

I closed the truck door and went back to my van. I was shivering now and grateful to slip on my sweatshirt. I put my gun back in my purse, slung the purse over my shoulder, and headed over to the cafe. Now, of course, when it did absolutely no damn good, the premonitions arrived, dark and ominous like a pair of buzzards perched on my shoulders. So I knew before I went inside the cafe that Wayne wouldn't be there.

I talked to the manager and to the cashier. They kept shaking their heads. No, neither of them remembered seeing Wayne, certainly not in the past hour or so. Before that they'd been busy and might not have noticed, then business had dropped off. "Damn fog," the manager said.

There was a pay phone outside by one of the restrooms. I dialed 911 and gave them the message that might get me in a whole lot of trouble but was sure to bring help. "There's an officer down," I said. "Newport Pier."

I hung up and took off for the beach. There was no point in giving Peggy bad news. She was due to call the police on my instructions pretty soon, and I might need the added weight of her fears to convince them that Wayne really was in danger.

The pier loomed overhead, jutting out in the ocean, vanishing in the fog. I headed around in back of one of the rest rooms toward the fishing shacks. The shacks are arranged in two rows facing each other, perpendicular to the beach. There's a board sidewalk in the middle, and old dories sit outside the shacks to serve as places to display the catch. As I remembered them, the shacks themself were used for storage, augmented by wooden lockers outside the doors. There are maybe ten on each side, windowless, the whole complex surrounded by wood pilings that are placed right up against the back of the shacks, walling them off. Up close the stench of fish was like a fist in the face.

Dories had been pulled up on the sand behind the little complex. There was no light except for the attenuated glow from the streetlamps. Sand sucked at my feet. I yelled for Wayne, but the crashing of water drowned out my voice. I tripped over the tongue of a boat trailer and went sprawling.

I would kill myself down here without a flashlight, and, anyway, I could hear sirens, distant but coming fast. I slogged back through the sand to the pavement and got to the cafe just as the first squad car screeched to a stop. Four more squad cars followed, plus a fire engine and a paramedic van. The commotion brought the cafe's customers outside to gawk.

The grim-faced sergeant who headed the charge wasn't pleased by my method of bringing the police, but Peggy's call had reached him on the way, so he listened to my explanation about the bombing and about Wayne's meeting down here. The other cops had gathered around. A couple of them knew Wayne and voiced their concern.

"If Wayne said he'd call, he would have—if he could," one said.

The other chimed in, "Yeah, and he wouldn't be worrying Peggy like this. She went through enough when he was dismantling bombs."

There was no more argument from the sergeant. He organized a search. The firemen volunteered to stay. Even a few customers from the cafe offered to join in. Armed with powerful halogen flashlights, one group headed south from the pier, another took off to search the pier itself, and the rest of us went to comb the shadows behind the shacks and the dory fleet.

Finding nothing there, we came back through the middle of the fishing shack plaza, probed around the old dories, and tried all the doors. Everything was locked up tight. Piles of fish scales gleamed, pearly gray, in my flashlight's beam. Fish blood had seeped into the boards, staining the wood, the stench permeating everything.

Oh, Jesus, let it just be fish blood.

Apprehension settled around my shoulders like a lead cloak. Wayne could be anywhere. God knows what we were missing in the dark. He might not even be here at all. He could have been taken out in a boat and dumped in the cold sea, or driven eastward to the hot, deserted stretches of sandy wasteland beyond Palm Springs.

An hour later, I was chilled to the bone, my energy draining away at an alarming rate. I was only two days out of the hospital, and every step reinforced the need to stop, to sit down, to *lie* down and rest. Somehow I kept going for another half-hour, until the sergeant ordered a halt in a tone that brooked no argument.

"We've done all we can in the dark," he said.

All I could think was that he wasn't the one who would have to tell Peggy we were giving up.

Everybody trudged wearily back to the cafe. A few more people had gathered, drawn like flies to carrion. The cafe manager offered free coffee, which the cops and firemen gulped gratefully before they took off. I slumped down in a booth, thankful for a place to sit and sip the hot liquid.

Customers hovered, avid for details. "Too bad they didn't find your friend," one said. "What do you think happened to him?"

"I don't know," I said, but my mind was working on a great many terrible possibilities.

"Somebody said you're a private eye." This came from a newcomer who had drifted over.

I admitted that I was, not really up to the what's-a-nice-lady-like-you routine.

But he just murmured, "Interesting," and stood there for a few seconds, looking down at me. He was slightly under six feet, but powerfully built. Long sandy hair was combed back and clubbed on the nape of a thick neck. More hair curled over the edge of the tank top he wore beneath a leather jacket that was adorned with metal studs and zippers. A gold earring gleamed in one ear. Just when his stare was beginning to annoy me, he gave me a little two-finger salute and drifted away.

I sat for another five minutes finishing my coffee. My back and neck hurt, the pain fiercely intense. There was a basket of crackers on the table. The last thing I wanted was food, but I ate a few saltines so I could take some Motrin.

Now that the drama was over, people were leaving and the manager was anxious to close up and go home. As for myself, I couldn't put off the call to Peggy Loftland any longer. I thanked the manager for the coffee and went out. I didn't want to use the pay phone. Too many of the curious still around, and, besides, it was too cold in the foggy night air. I would use the car phone in the van.

In the parking lot, the lights had gone off. Next to my Astro van, Wayne's old Toyota looked even more ominously abandoned in the murky darkness. I took out my car keys, remembering as I did so that I'd left the van unlocked when I rushed off to look for Wayne. Even with the cops swarming around, some bold thief could have helped himself to a few good-

ies. I heaved a sigh of relief as I climbed in and saw
the obvious things were still there: radio, car phone—

My relief died stillborn, and my blood froze as I
saw just a flicker of movement reflected in the rearview mirror. Enough to know somebody was behind
me a split second before a powerful arm snaked out,
wrapped around my throat, and slammed me back
in the seat.

Pain zapped my tender neck muscles like a stun-
gun. I felt my purse sliding off my lap. At the same
time I caught a glimpse of slicked-back hair and the
glint of a gold earring stud in the rearview mirror.

I clawed instinctively at the arm around my neck.
My brain issued other orders: Go for his eyes, grab
the purse strap, get to the thirty-eight. But I couldn't
touch the man's head and my purse was gone, down
on the floor by my feet. Out of reach, the god-
damned gun was always out of reach. Then it didn't
matter. A wicked little twenty-five caliber Beretta was
in the man's hand, the metal snout pressed hard
against my right temple.

"Hey, Miss P.I.," the man said.

I stopped fighting. No use anyway. I was about ten
seconds away from losing consciousness due to the
cruel pressure on my windpipe.

"That's better."

He eased up and let me take a shallow breath.

"Tell you what we're gonna do," he said. "We're
gonna sit here real peaceful and quiet until everybody over there at the cafe goes home."

"And then what?" I asked hoarsely.

"Why, then I'm going to take you to see your buddy Wayne. Won't that be nice?"

SEVENTEEN

A FILM OF SALT SPRAY and fog on the van's big windows turned the world beyond distant and surreal. Misty halos ringed the streetlamps, and taillights of departing cars were red smears echoed in the neon reflections on the wet pavement. Earring released me long enough to run a hard hand over my body in a quick, businesslike search, then pinioned me again, his arm just at the tops of my breasts. I figured my lower arms were about ten inches short of being able to reach the horn.

"What happens if somebody comes over?" I asked.

"First I kill you then I blow his head off," my captor said.

As it turns out, this was not a problem. Not a single person came to check on me. They all got in their cars and drove away.

About then I guess Earring got tired of holding me in place against the seat. Well, it was an awkward position for him, all hunched over like that. He ordered me to put my hands on top of my head and keep them there. Meanwhile his gun stayed pressed against my temple with him close enough so I could smell his beery breath and high-pitched body odor.

"We'll give it another five minutes," he said.

"Is Wayne all right?" I asked.

"Oh, yeah, he's great."

"Look, Wayne's a reasonable man, and I'm easy to get along with too. Let's talk. I'm sure we can deal—"

"Can it." He sounded bored and edgy. He shifted around, his leather jacket making a whispery creak.

I slid a foot out cautiously and felt the solid lump of my purse on the floor. No way I could make a dive for it now, but at some point—

"Ah, fuck this," Earring said. "We're gonna get out now. You do it right, just like I tell you, or you're gonna be real dead."

He took his arm away and told me to move over to the passenger seat and open the sliding door. It was now or never on reaching my gun. Thinking about it, deciding, I hesitated for only a second. Too long. He grabbed my arm and hauled me across to the passenger side. Prodded me with the Beretta.

"Now! Do it!" he said.

I pulled open the big wide door. It was easy for him to leap down and yank me out in a couple of swift movements, leaving my purse in the van with my gun inside.

Naturally.

He closed the door, then clamped a hand on my arm, stuck the Beretta in my back, and marched me across the asphalt back toward the cafe.

I was in considerable pain from his original attack and the subsequent manhandling. Good thing I'd taken the Motrin. Only I thought maybe I should have swallowed a whole handful of the little suckers.

He made a right turn and steered me onto the boardwalk that ran down the middle of the rows of fishing shacks, then about midway, he threaded his way in between a couple of old dories, shoving me ahead of him. It was very dark. Out in back the fishing boats loomed, black on black, and surf crashed like thunder. I hoped he'd trip over something, maybe break his neck, but no such luck.

Well, I could fake a stumble, drive an elbow into his midrift and hope his finger wasn't wrapped around the trigger.

Too late.

Again.

He rapped on a door, said, "Open up."

"Zack?" somebody said from inside.

"Who the hell do you think? Let me in."

The door opened. It was blacker inside than out. Earring—Zack—Zackery Pellissier, ex-U.S.M.C., I presumed—shoved me inside. The door thumped shut behind us.

"Jesus, what took you so long?" the man demanded. A pencil beam came on and I got an impression of bulk and bushy hair and tattoos.

"Relax, Turk," Zack said. "It took a while for everybody to clear out."

Turk leaned over to flip a wall switch. A bare light bulb, about a twenty-watter, went on in the ceiling. I remembered the interior of the individual shacks being small, about ten by twelve feet, more like storage closets. This one was bigger, maybe two spaces put together. One side was covered with crammed shelves. There were stacks of mucky plastic bins and a lot of metal buckets, piles of coiled fishing line bristling with hooks. The air was close and stuffy, the stench amazingly strong.

Wayne lay over in one corner next to a big chest-type freezer, adhesive tape wound around his hands and feet and a wide strip of tape covering his mouth. His eyes were open, blinking in the sudden light. He made a muffled sound of recognition and regret when he saw me. One side of his face was a pulpy mess, his hair matted with blood. There was blood on his shirt too, big stains on the front and more streaks down his sleeves.

I tried to pull loose from Zack. He held me for a couple of seconds just to show me who was boss, then let me go.

"Try anything stupid," he warned, "and your buddy's the first one I shoot."

I rushed over and dropped down by Wayne.

"You damn fool," I muttered, anger and relief and fear all mixed together in my voice. "I told you to wait for me."

I reached for the tape on his mouth, but Zack said sharply, "Let him alone."

"What difference does it make?" I asked. "Nobody's around to hear us."

Of course I hoped there would be somebody soon. My van was still out there, sitting next to Wayne's truck. Surely the Newport police would be checking back—some of Wayne's friends still worried about him—and see the van.

"*I* can hear you," Zack said. "So just sit there and keep your mouth shut."

I sat on the floor, touching Wayne's arm, trying to signal reassurance. Hell, who was I kidding? Wayne's shirt was torn and I could see purpling flesh on his shoulder. He must have been here, with Turk keeping him quiet, all the time we searched outside.

It amazed me that Turk could keep *himself* quiet that long. The man was clearly wired, the pupils huge in his shiny, pale blue eyes. He looked like a gorilla who had spent the last ten years over at Ultimate Fitness working out on the weight machines. Make that a hairless gorilla. From the density of the uncombed black hair on his head I thought he ought to have some on his body too. Maybe he shaved it off. He wore jeans and black boots and a black tank top to show off his muscles and the veritable canvas of tattoos—birds, snakes, twiny flowers, and God knows what-all—that covered his long, apelike arms.

His glance jittered over to me and Wayne, then back to Zack. "Did you call him?"

"Yeah, he's on his way," Zack said.

"Let me guess," I said. "Your old pal, Tony Vero."

"Shit." Turk was clearly taken aback. "She knows about Tony?"

"So what?" Zack said, but it shook him a little too. "How do you know about Tony and us?"

"The fight at Cook's Corner."

"What fight?" Turk asked.

Zack studied me for a moment, a grudging flicker of respect in his eyes. "Coupla years ago. You weren't there."

"But *you* were," I said to Zack. "And if I know about your connection to Tony, you can be sure a lot of other people do too."

"*He* didn't." Zack gestured to Wayne. "And it didn't sound as though any of those cops tonight did either. So who does that leave?" He grinned. "Just the gook, huh?"

"No," I said quickly. "Danny's my gofer, that's all. I wrote everything up and put a copy in my safety deposit box."

"Yeah? Well, maybe we'll have to blow up the goddamn bank—right after we take out the gook, that is. Fix her up, Turk. I still got stuff to do before Tony gets here."

About a million things flashed through my head. All the things I should have done differently, like studying karate or tai chi or picking a different career in the first place. I planned and discarded a dozen wild schemes involving the creative use of bait buckets and fishing line. Reality and Zack's Beretta aimed at Wayne's head kept me sitting right there while Turk picked up a roll of adhesive tape, came over, grabbed my arm, and yanked me up.

He wound off a length of Johnson and Johnson half-inch, used his teeth to tear it. I felt a dismal wave of deja vu. Adhesive tape seemed to be the manacle of choice for unimaginative criminals these days. Worse, it was the second time recently that the damn stuff had been used on me.

I steeled myself, but I still went a little faint at the tearing shock of pain in my tender shoulder muscles when he pulled my arms behind my back. All I could do was put as much resistance as possible against the tape to try and generate a little slack. I did the same thing when he shoved me down on the floor beside Wayne and taped my ankles.

"Now, don't you go nowhere." Turk gave me a luminously evil grin and a pat on the cheek—the touch about like being kissed by a rattlesnake.

Zack waited for him at the door. "Listen, take it easy on the shit now. You wanna slow down, stay frosty."

"Easy for you," Turk said, joining him. "I'm the one in here smelling this stink—Jesus, I'll never eat a fucking fish again."

Turk flipped off the light switch. I heard the door open and close. The light came back on. Turk prowled around the small room and stopped beside the freezer. A blue nylon gym bag and leather jacket lay on top. He dipped into the jacket pocket and brought out a small zip-lock bag that contained some white powder. Tapped a little on the back of his hand. Sniffed. Rubbed the residue on his gums.

"So Tony gets here. And then what?" I asked.

He gave me a bright, sly look. "We'll have a party. A real blast."

Outside I heard an engine start. So much for my hope of the police seeing my van and getting suspicious, because I was certain I recognized the sound of my Astro van driving away. Not far, I was sure. Just someplace nearby out of sight. Wayne made a little noise and looked up at me, eyes full of frustration. Maybe he'd been thinking along the same track.

Turk put away his cocaine, knocked out a riffle on the freezer, really juiced now.

Which one of them had killed Sandy? I'd bet on Zack. He had a kind of dangerous attraction that some women find irresistible. If Sandy had been mixed up with somebody like him, it might explain why she never introduced her lover to her friends. Of the two, however, I thought Turk might be the easier to get to, and even that was a longshot.

"You guys really are nuts," I said. "You're leaving tracks a blind man could follow. I meant what I said about telling the cops—the Santa Ana police, not the ones down here."

Turk tapped out a tinny drum beat on the metal shelving, picked up a box, put it down, opened another, took out a fishing lure with a hook attached, and twirled it—a big, feathered one, all shades of green and yellow.

"Think about yourself here, Turk. Cut us loose, and we'll help you make a deal. Wayne's still got a lot of clout in the sheriff's office."

Turk collected a couple more fishing lures, saying nothing, thinking it over—I hoped.

"You've got a hell of a lot to trade, Turk. You can give the cops your explosives supplier. You can finger who killed Sandy—" *Assuming you didn't do it yourself, or, if you did, you can lie and make it stick.* "You can give them anything that connects this to Sam Newley."

Turk hunkered down in front of me and looked at me as though I had gone completely round the bend. "What the *fuck* are you talking about? We ain't killed nobody—yet—not for a while."

He held the big lure by the hook next to my face, and the feathers brushed my cheek. I shrunk a little closer to Wayne.

"Sandy Renkowski," I said. "She worked with Tony. Blond, very pretty—"

He tossed the first lure on the floor, held up another, bright orange. Tossed that aside too.

"Fix yourself up, you wouldn't be a bad-looking chick." Another lure, a blue puffball with a wickedly sharp barb of shiny metal. "You talk too damn much though. I don't like talkers."

A glimmer of a grin and then he moved—very fast. Seizing my hair, he pulled me down on the floor, clamped his knees around my head, grabbed my right ear and drove the fishing hook through the soft fleshy lobe.

I DIDN'T PASS OUT, exactly. Reality just rearranged itself for a few seconds as a white hot streak of pain shot up into my head via my jaw. Well, I'd always *known* people were lying when they said it didn't hurt to get your ears pierced.

I came out of it to muffled noise and thumps— Wayne swearing behind his gag and banging his knees and heels on the floor. Blood ran from my ear into my mouth, warm and salty.

Turk quieted Wayne with an indifferent kick in his ribs, then stood there staring down at me, contemplating his handiwork with a loony smile.

I spat blood and hitched myself back against Wayne, struggling to sit up. "Sadistic bastard—"

"Shut up," he said, listening.

Voices outside. I was prepared to scream my head off and take the consequences, but I recognized Zack's voice. Turk sprang over to turn off the light. Zack said, "Open up," and I heard the door open and close while Tony Vero was saying, "This better be good, Zack. I have to get up and go to work in the—"

Then Turk flipped the light back on, and Tony broke off and stood there with his mouth open, gaze riveted on my face.

"Hey, Tone," Turk said. "Not bad, huh?"

"Jesus," Tony said faintly.

"What do you think? Needs another one in the other ear, huh?"

"Knock it off, Turk," Zack said.

"What the *hell* is going on?" Tony asked. "Have you gone totally batshit crazy?"

Somehow I thought old Tone had hit the situation square on the head.

EIGHTEEN

"WELCOME TO THE PARTY, Tony," I said. "Or as your cretin friend here puts it, the big blast."

"Shut her up," Zack ordered.

Turk had to fumble around for the tape, so I had time to add, "Better make sure you're one of the hosts and not an attendee."

Then Turk ripped off a couple of inches of tape and reached for me. I turned my head away, not because I knew the resistance would do any good—and it didn't—but so I could quickly spread some saliva and blood around my lip area. When Turk slapped the tape over my mouth, the tape stuck on the edges, but not where I had licked. Wayne caught what I'd done, but he didn't seem all that cheered by my small victory.

"Christ," Tony said, aghast. "What the fuck is wrong with you two? First off, I ask you to scare the broad like you did the Calder woman, but instead you send a live bomb—"

"Hey," Zack said. "Don't blame me. Turk made the delivery."

"Yeah," Turk said. "And I thought, why dick around? Do the job right. Know your problem,

Tone? You've gone soft sittin' around that fruity office. You oughta loosen up. Have some fun.''

"*Fun?*" Tony gestured to us. "This is your idea of fun?''

"No," Zack said patiently. "*This* is a situation. See, old Wayne over there comes looking for a buy. Came recommended, seemed okay, but I smelled a setup. We're out on the pier, right? Fishing on the pier. I let him think I bought his story, told him we're going to stay out there till the crowds thin, then we'll check with our people, have them meet us. He's nervous, but we got him between us, so what can he do? The fog rolls in. Turk used to work here a coupla years back so we know that the fish merchants close up early when it gets foggy.''

"Greek son of a bitch," Turk put in. "He fired me, but he forgot I had a key.''

"So we bring Wayne here," Zack said. "Lean on him a little. He doesn't say much, and he's got no I.D. in his wallet, but hey, his truck's out there, easy to spot once everybody went home, and the key's in his pocket. We got his registration; we know where he lives.

"So he tells us some things. Like he's an ex-cop, ex-bomb squad, doing a favor for the department, he says, a little undercover work. Sounds reasonable. We're waiting around for everything to close up, gonna take him back out to the end of the pier and pop him. Then *she* shows up." He gestured toward me. "I go to check it out, and pretty soon the whole damn Newport police force comes running."

All during Zack's recitation I could feel the blood dripping from my ear down inside my shirt. Pain pulsed up into my jaw. I had a feeling, however, judging from Turk's sly grin, that pretty soon I was going to have something a whole lot worse to worry about. And Tony's response didn't reassure me at all.

"Oh God. Oh shit." Tony clenched and unclenched his ugly hands. "Do you have any idea what you are doing here? You are fucking up my entire life."

Come to think of it, Tony *was* looking kind of seedy. In the squalid light his skin was pale, even a little green. He'd been losing sleep, witness the bags under his eyes. Even the casually elegant pale yellow shirt and navy slacks were totally wrong with the old leather motorcycle jacket and scuffed boots.

"Funny," Zack said. "A little while ago it was, 'You gotta help me out, Zack. This is my big chance. Ol' Sam's depending on me to smooth out all the bumps and take out the garbage.'"

"I never said I wanted you to hurt anybody," Tony said.

"Yeah, well, things got out of control. It happens. All you can do is make the best of it."

"Well, then fucking *do* it," Tony said. "This is your mess. You handle it and leave me out."

"Afraid I can't do that." Zack pulled the Beretta from his pocket and pointed it at Tony.

Tony stared at the gun in disbelief. "What the fuck are you *doing?*"

"Afraid you're part of the problem, Tony," Zack said.

"Now wait a minute—" Tony darted frightened glances between Zack and Turk, who was over by the freezer taking something from his jacket.

"I remember how bent you got after that little fracas at Cook's Corner," Zack said. "Went whining to your big county whip boss. That was just some wimpy assault charge. What would you do if it was murder?"

"I wouldn't *do* anything—"

"Sure you would," Turk said. "You'd sing like a fucking canary."

He turned from the freezer, holding what looked to me from my vantage point on the floor like an old sock filled with something—probably sand.

"No—" Tony's head whipped back and forth, looking for a way out, even shooting a beseeching glance at Wayne and me. "No, wait. Listen—"

He put out his hands, stumbled backward a few steps. Turk timed it just right, moved in, and swung the sock. A solid *thunk* as it connected, and Tony went down.

Turk used up the rest of the adhesive tape on him. I thought if I ever got out of here, I might buy some Johnson and Johnson stock. Meanwhile Zack went over and opened the gym bag, took out a small, rectangular device, and pushed some buttons. Wayne drew in a shuddering breath at the sight of it, confirming my worst suspicions.

Finished with Tony, Turk paused beside me, grinning his nasty grin, flicking the fishing lure in my ear. This was about like being touched by a cattle prod.

"Too bad," Turk said. "Might've had us some fun."

"Stop screwing around," Zack said sharply. His gaze swept around the room, passing over us with the impersonal appraisal of a hunter staking out lambs for the wolves. "Guess that's everything."

"Let's do it," Turk said. Nothing impersonal about the brutish glee on his face as he followed Zack to the door.

They switched off the light, went out, and locked the door behind them. In the sudden darkness something glowed red on top of the freezer. Zack had left the gym bag open, and I knew I was seeing an LED readout, and that the rectangular device was a timer.

I blinked frantically, trying to make out the numbers, remembering the sound of the bomb going off in my office, that clap of thunder splitting the world asunder. One and a half ounces of C-4, Wayne had estimated. How much was in the gym bag? My skin contracted with terror, anticipating the blast that would be unleashed any second now...

No, that was stupid. There would be some time. Enough for Zack and Turk to get clear, probably enough so they could get off the peninsula.

I couldn't so much hear their footsteps outside over the muted roar of surf as feel their weight on the boardwalk, the movement transmitted into the wood of the floor. About the time my eyes adjusted enough to read the timer, I heard the muffled but unmistakable roar of two Harleys rumbling to life outside.

14:12, the timer said, but even as I read it the thing counted backward: *14:11, 14:10.*

Frantically I scrubbed the edge of the tape that covered my mouth against my shoulder—the left side, opposite my fishing lure earring. I wriggled my hands, too. My stomach roiled from the putrid smells, and sweat greased my body.

13:58.

Twelve damn seconds just to get the tape on my face loosened. Time enough to think about Danny. He'd be safe at home now. Surely they didn't know where he lived. But when he went to the office in a couple of hours ...

Another ten to get my mouth freed enough to croak, "Wayne—Jesus, Wayne—"

My hands were still firmly bound. I leaned down, nuzzling around, finding his face.

"Hold still," I said. I located the edge of the tape that was plastered over his mouth. "Gonna hurt," I warned, then got the edge between my teeth and gave a quick yank.

He yelped, cursed, then muttered thickly, "God— Delilah—"

13:18.

"I'm going to get you loose," I said. "You can do something, can't you?"

"Have to."

"Roll over a little so I can get to your hands."

Even in the darkness I could make out vague out-lines now. Tony was an inert lump a few feet away. Wayne moved, moaning as he did so.

"The son of a bitch—think he cracked my rib—"

I leaned over him, hunting for his wrists, sup-pressing a scream as my skewered ear banged into his shoulder. I'd seen Turk use his teeth on the adhesive tape to start a tear point. Surely I could chew my way through the stuff.

I bit into the edge. Easy enough for Turk to work on one ply and have the use of his hands to finish the job. But there was five or six layers wound around Wayne's wrists. And the timer kept counting down.

12:32.

I chewed faster. Flexed my own wrists.

12:24.

The taste of the adhesive mixed with the taste of blood. My ear was bleeding again. Count your blessings, I told myself. Turk could just as easily have used the big lure with the yellow and green feathers.

I stopped chewing and sat up.

"What?" Wayne said. "Can't you do it?"

"Taking forever. Got to find something else—"

There had to be all kinds of useful objects in the room, in the boxes on the shelves. First priority though—no more working in the dark.

Getting up was the hard part. Try it sometime, hands taped behind your back, feet taped together, if you don't believe me.

11:54.

Once I was up, at least it was a straight shot to the door with the malevolent eye of the timer as a guide. I began hopping, each jarring shock sending a painful jolt up my body.

Five hops.

"Delilah—"

"Almost there."

Two more.

11:22.

I pictured Turk flipping on the light. The left side of the door. I stumbled against the wall, brushed my head around, and bumped the switch.

Sickly light flooded the room, but, God, it seemed bright as sunrise to me. I plotted a straight line to the metal shelves. Four hops. I panted with the effort, swaying to keep my balance. One more jump, but this time my torso was too far forward.

I fell, close enough to the shelving so my right arm skimmed down against it. A sharp corner grooved my skin, drawing a fiery line. The heavily laden shelf lurched as I hit the floor.

"Delilah?" Wayne called in alarm.

"I'm okay."

I wasn't. I hurt all over. Between my ear and the cut on my arm I was beginning to look like a refugee from a slaughter house. I *had* to get up, and right now—

10:38, 10:37

—or did I?

About two feet from the floor a shelf had been carelessly attached to the front upright support, leaving a quarter-inch protrusion. The damned thing glistened with my blood so I knew how sharp it was.

"The time," Wayne said. "Get moving, for God's sake."

"I am."

I struggled up on my knees, turned, and put my wrists against the support, sliding them down and using the shelf edge to saw the tape.

10:07.

"Delilah?" Wayne said desperately. "Talk to me."

"Wait—almost—"

My arms kept slipping out of position. I stifled a cry as I miscalculated and nicked my wristbone.

I found the edge again. Sawed faster.

9:08.

The tape gave. I flexed my wrists frantically, never mind the pain jolting up into my shoulders. And then, suddenly, I was free.

"Got it!" I sang out.

With the use of my hands it was easy to clamber up, using the shelving for balance. The first thing I encountered was the box of fishing lures—the big feathered ones with the razor-sharp barb. I took one and used it to slice the tape on my ankles.

I gave a jubilant whoop. "Wayne! We're going to be okay. Soon as I get you loose—"

I scanned the shelves. Something much better than the barbed lure lay on an upper shelf—a boning knife. I grabbed it and ran over—well, hobbled over is a more accurate description—to Wayne.

8:14.

"We got it made," I said as I quickly cut his wrists free, then worked on his ankles. "Lots of time. Piece of cake."

Only just then, looking at Wayne, my confident words sounded hollow. He lay there, pasty gray, clammy with sweat, massaging hands swollen fat as sausages. Alarm bells dinned in the back of my head.

"Come on," I said.

I slipped an arm under his shoulders. He groaned as I eased him to a sitting position.

"Wayne? You can do something, right? I can help you, God knows I will, but—"

He was shaking his head. "Before—didn't want to tell you. Have to now. Delilah—can't do it—"

"What do you mean? You can't do what?"

"I can't disarm the bomb."

7:43, 7:42, 7:41.

Two whole seconds for his words to sink in.

"Uh uh," I said. "No, no. Take a minute. Get your bearings. Let me help you—"

I took over massaging his hands, but he kept shaking his head.

"Goddammit, Wayne, don't you crap out on me. In about seven minutes we're going to be so much human confetti decorating the boardwalk."

"Don't you think *I* know that—my God." He pulled his hands away and held them up. "What do you see here? Two hands, ten numb fingers, right? I see at least twenty. I got a few thumps on the head before you got here, Delilah. Minor concussion, I think—I hope. But I'm in no condition to mess around with high explosives. Trust me."

I sank back on my heels, dismay lumping in my stomach, remembering distinctly what double vision was like. "What do we do then?"

"The door—any way you can get out?"

I shook my head. "Keyed deadbolt. I'm not strong enough to break it down." I glanced over at Tony, still unconscious, maybe with a lot worse concussion than Wayne. "If I had enough time I suppose I could carve around the lock—"

We both looked at the timer.

6:39.

"Christ on the cross," Wayne said.

"Amen. Where does that leave us?"

"Only one option," Wayne said. "You. You have to disarm the bomb."

NINETEEN

6:01

I stared at that winking red eye, horrified, and said faintly, "There's got to be another way."

"Think of one."

5:59.

"Wayne—"

5:58.

"I'll talk you through it," Wayne said. "Step by step. You have to do it, Delilah."

I drew a shuddering breath. "All right. Tell me."

"First I want you to describe the device to me, exactly."

I went over to the freezer and gingerly pulled open the gym bag.

"A great big lump of something like gray putty," I said. "Plastic explosive?"

"You bet."

5:18.

"Two wires coming out of that," I said. "The wires are attached to the timer."

"Can you see what's on the other end of the leg wires?"

"No."

"What color are the wires?"

"Kind of an olive drab."

"Figures," Wayne said. "Military. What we got is probably a blasting cap inserted down in the C-4. First thing is to cut the wires to the timer."

"Can I use the knife?"

"If you have to, but look around. See if you can find some wire cutters."

4:49.

I rummaged quickly through the stuff on the workbench.

"How about needle-nosed pliers?" Wayne asked. "Or—Christ, Delilah, come over here." He pawed at his pants pocket with numb fingers.

I went quickly to kneel beside him.

"Nail clippers," he said. "In my pocket. Almost forgot."

I took them out.

"All right," he said. "Now go clip the wires."

"Just like that?" Why had I thought it was warm in the stuffy room? My teeth would start chattering any minute. "Which one first? Should I bring the bag over so you can see?"

"No, don't move it—too risky. The sequence shouldn't matter, unless they got really tricky."

Unless.

I went back to the gym bag.

3:51.

My hand shook. I grasped the wrist with my other hand and took a couple of deep breaths.

"What did you mean if they got tricky?" I asked.

"Never mind. Just for Chrissake *do it*."

The red eye of the timer winked at me: *3:33, 3:32*.

I snipped one wire, then the other.

The timer blinked out.

My legs felt as though somebody was pouring sand down the insides of them. I leaned against the freezer to keep from falling.

"I did it, Wayne." Exhilaration shot through me, potent as brandy. "I cut the little suckers."

"Don't get too excited," Wayne said grimly. "You're not finished. All you've done is disconnect the timer. We've still got a blasting cap to deal with."

"Can't it wait? Fishing boats go out early. When somebody comes, we can send for the bomb squad."

"No," Wayne said. "It cannot wait. A radio signal can set the damn thing off. A walkie-talkie. One of my buddies from the Newport police swings back here because he's still worried about me, uses his radio, and that's all she wrote."

My elation fizzled. "All right. Tell me."

"Nothing tricky. Just lift the cap out, carefully."

I did it, my mind skittering around, maybe because I didn't want to face what could happen if that stray signal zoned in on the blasting cap I was extracting from the C-4.

Turk hadn't killed Sandy, hadn't even known who she was. Maybe Zack had, but I didn't think so. I thought the two of them were just who they seemed: parts of Tony Vero's dangerous second life that had gotten out of control. So maybe Tony was the mur-

derer after all—or Sam himself—or the boyfriend I
hadn't found...

"All right," I said. "The cap's out. Now what?"

"Now we try to isolate it. See that book? Up on
the shelf."

I took down a thick catalog.

"Open it up, put the cap inside, and close it,"
Wayne said.

I did just that. "Anything else we can do?"

"Wait." Wayne said. "And maybe pray a little."

WE SPENT ANOTHER tense hour before somebody
came, an astonished fisherman who took some con-
vincing that this wasn't a macabre joke. That ac-
complished, things went quickly.

Police. The bomb squad. Paramedics.

Fresh, untainted air.

I let myself be taken to the hospital with Wayne
and Tony, but I resisted all doctors until I knew
Wayne was all right, that Danny was under police
protection, and that a SWAT team awaited Turk and
Zack at my office. Considering the state of my
blood-stained clothes, this was quite an accomplish-
ment.

I even managed to call Rita and ask her to please
go down to Newport Pier to secure my van and, assuming Turk and Zack were not thieves as well as
assassins, to please collect my purse.

Finally, I found myself in a curtained cubicle with
an ER nurse who checked me out, then turned me

over to Dr. Forbisher, who was female, my age, and fashionably slender in her green lab coat. She examined me, observing my decorated ear and pronouncing it "Not the neatest piercing job I ever saw."

She clipped off the barbed end of the lure with some cutters and pulled the thing out. I noted she wore some silver unicorns in her own ears. She said I needed a couple of stitches, numbed the lobe, cleaned, and sutured.

"Now's the time to tell me if you want the opening completely closed," she said. "What do you think? There'll probably be a scar anyway."

"Do I have to wear the lure?" I asked.

She grinned, then took out one of her silver unicorns, disinfected it, and put it in place.

LIEUTENANT BRADY was waiting outside the Emergency Room. I got a sudden foreboding of bad news and said, "Danny?"

"He's fine," Brady said. "We got the bikers. They were doing a little early morning recon cruise outside your office. Of course they claim they were only out for a spin and just happened to have two guns and a half pound of C-4 with them."

"There's another name I can give you, their supplier at Camp Pendleton. But if you expect to take me down to make a statement right now, you'd better have a bedroll in your office. I'm beat."

"No, it can wait. Wayne Loftland filled me in."
An awkward pause, during which I swear he shuf-
fled his feet. "Thought you might need a ride
home," he said gruffly.

I stared at him, too amazed to do more than
mumble, "Thanks," and follow him out to his car.

RITA AND FARLEY must have returned my van, because it was parked in front of the condo and my
purse was inside my house with everything in order.

I managed a shower, then fell into bed to sleep
soundly for six hours. I awakened to the smell of
coffee and baking bread. Rita had let herself in and
was chopping up red and green peppers and mush-
rooms for an omelet. For filling my house with these
heavenly aromas, I could even forgive her the oat
bran in the bread.

Once she had me eating, she gave my unicorn a
critical look and said, "I could've done it with a
needle and ice cube. All you had to do was ask."

I wolfed down my eggs and sipped some coffee.
"Thanks for bringing the van back. Any calls while
I was asleep?"

"I don't suppose you'd consider going back to bed
for a while?"

"Rita, it's the middle of the afternoon. Anyway, I
can't. I have things to do."

"Wonder why I'm not surprised."

Along with some clients who wanted to know if
this time they really should start looking for another

investigator, she listed among my callers Danny, Harry, Harvey, Bobbi, Lieutenant Brady, and, finally, Erik.

"Erik?"

"Yeah. As in Erik Lundstrom, the guy you never hear from."

I felt my cheeks get pink, and this time I couldn't blame it on the sunburn. "I'd better get busy. Just leave the dishes. I'll do them later."

"No, I'll clean up. You go make your calls."

I took the portable phone into my bedroom, sat on the unmade bed, propped myself up against some pillows, and considered who I should call first. Who was I kidding? I called Erik at home and was put straight through.

"Delilah? I had to go to Sacramento early this morning. When I was on my way home from the airport, I heard what happened on the car radio. I went straight to the hospital, but you were already gone. Are you sure you're all right?"

"Positive."

"The newscast said the police caught the bombers. And they've arrested Sam Newley's assistant. Does that mean Sam's no longer a murder suspect?"

"Not yet. There's still an awful lot of loose ends to tie up."

He sighed. "I see. Well, I'm afraid I'm not going to be much help. I intended to call you anyway to tell you I haven't turned up anything suspicious. There're plenty of development deals around the county, but all of them are on the public record."

Somehow I was not surprised to hear this. "Okay. Thanks for looking into it. Erik? After I finish this case, we need to get together and talk about some things."

"Things," he said dryly. "Sure. Let's do that. Meantime, will you please stay out of hospitals?"

I promised I'd try, disconnected, and called Lieutenant Brady. During my six-hour nap Tony Vero had been awake and, promised immunity from prosecution, was even now singing his little heart out just as Turk had predicted.

Tony confessed to setting up Sandy Renkowski for the park fund theft and to hiring me to make the setup look legit. It seems, however, that none of this had anything to do with Sandy's connection to Bobbi. I had given Tony too much credit on that score. He was neither intelligent nor sly enough to plot such subterfuge.

"Would you believe Vero was dipping his own sticky little fingers into the fund?" Brady said. "Somebody in the office noticed discrepancies; Tony panicked and began looking around for a scapegoat."

"Sandy?"

"Bingo. The new girl on the block."

"So Bobbi's letter bomb scare was not connected to the theft?"

"Nope. Coincidence. Just like I tried to tell you."

Tony also insisted that Sam Newley never knew anything about the letter bombs, either about Bobbi's threat or about my live one. I wasn't sure I believed this, but since there was no proof of Sam's complicity, we would have to take Tony's word.

"Jeez," I said. "Do you suppose Tony ever once considered just doing his job the old fashioned way?"

"It's the mind set," Brady said wisely. "Once a street punk, always a street punk. Now, the part you won't be too happy to hear: Vero denies that he killed Miss Renkowski or asked any of his buddies to do it."

"And you believe him?"

"Yeah," Brady said. "I do. More important, so does the D.A. Vero's a low life and a weasel, but I don't think he's a murderer. Unless you can come up with some new evidence, we're going with Bobbi Calder. Sorry," he added, surprising me for the second time that day.

After hanging up, I seriously considered crawling back into bed, pulling the covers over my head, and staying there for a week or two. I had been blown up, pushed around, stabbed with a fish hook, and forced to become a bomb expert in one agonizing lesson.

All this and my client was still charged with murder one.

Hell.

I allowed myself a full minute of gloomy self-pity, then climbed out of bed and got dressed. The least I could do was go tell Bobbi the bad news in person.

TWENTY

WHILE I DRESSED, Rita stuck her head in to say good-bye, and I fielded two phone calls. One was from Harvey Klein, who asked if I had uncovered anything that had not been turned over to the D.A. He sounded as though he expected to be told no.

The other call was from Ellen Klein. She seemed sober enough, curbing her strident excitement and not slurring a single syllable as she prattled on about seeing a TV report on the bombers' arrest and how surely now Bobbi would be free, wouldn't she?

"Ellen, I'm sorry. You'll have to ask Harvey about it," I said. "But don't get your hopes up."

"They haven't dropped the charges against Bobbi?"

"No. I'm sure Harvey will fill you in. I really do have to go now."

She turned subdued and apologetic. "Of course. Yes. Sorry. I don't want to keep you."

I thought about calling Harvey back, but to hell with it. I was getting damn tired of being in the middle of a situation that was no concern of mine. So instead I phoned Bobbi to say I was coming down and then, finally, I got around to calling Danny.

I could hear the relief in his voice when I assured him I was only slightly the worse for wear. "I don't have time for details now. How far did you get with Sandy's address book and her phone calls?"

"There's about a month's worth of phone billings left to do and T through Z in the address book plus a little backtracking to cover numbers that didn't answer. I stopped working on it because I just assumed—you still don't know who killed Sandy?"

"I'm afraid not, Danny. Could you get back on this, please?"

"Sure," he said. He promised to stay and finish up and call me if he turned up anything.

Rush-hour traffic was just getting down to some serious stopping and going when I left my condo to drive to Laguna Beach. Construction on the Santa Ana Freeway just added to the confusion. Concrete blocking topped with plywood created a barricade that screened the activity in the middle of the road. Driving next to the barricade gives you the continuous feeling that you will be crashing into a wall at any minute. I got in the middle lane and stayed there, convinced more than ever that the whole project is some kind of survival test.

I had to keep my wits about me as traffic sprang along like some kind of organic slinky, but I still had plenty of time to think about Sandy's death.

With all the complications of the bombing and covert development deals swept away, I was left with the conviction I had felt that day standing in Sandy's apartment: Sandy's murder had been a crime of passion—lust, hate, fear—some combination of these emotions erupting into the rage that caused the murderer to stab Sandy with enough force to kill her and to keep on stabbing the dying woman until the rage was spent.

Sandy's lover was the obvious candidate. Maybe they had a fight. Maybe Sandy had tried to break off the relationship. Danny might still turn up something, but the possibility looked pretty remote. Sandy's apartment building still seemed my best shot. Running on the edge of pain and exhaustion and overwhelmed with the sheer amount of work I was facing, I had let her neighbors put me off. In-depth questioning was certainly in order, I decided as I finally made my exit onto Laguna Canyon Road. Plus I would make a concerted effort to speak to every single resident in the building.

Sandy's boyfriend might even be one of those hard bodies I'd met at the pool, their casual meeting amidst the beer and sunshine for some reason turned secretive, dark, and deadly.

I considered other approaches to the investigation as I drove into Laguna and climbed the hillside street to Bobbi's house, especially a trip to Boston for a talk with Sandy's uncooperative father.

I parked and got out. The sun was sinking into the cottony fogbank that lay just offshore. Already the air felt cool and damp. Another misty, chilly night ahead. Thank God I wouldn't be spending it in a fishing shack at Newport Pier.

Bobbi answered the door with a drink in her hand. She wore an oversized pistachio knit top and black stirrup pants. She was barefoot. Strands of heavy graying hair escaped from clumsily anchored tortoiseshell combs.

"Dinner," she said, indicating the glass. She looked ten years older, her face ravaged with despair.

"Harvey called you?" I guessed.

"Oh, yes. Twice, in fact. This morning when he heard what had happened to you and that people had been arrested. I had a couple of hours there when I hoped this nightmare would be over. Amazing. Then, of course, he called again..."

She led the way, unsteadily, into the living room which was luminous with pearly light. "A drink?" she said. "Please, help yourself. I'm not really up to bartending."

"No, thanks," I said.

"Then sit."

She gestured to the big sectional sofa and sank down in one corner. A half-dozen framed pictures stood on the marble coffee table. I switched on a hanging lamp and recognized among the photos the one of Bobbi and Lynne with the child that was Sandy between them, and the group shot including Harvey and Sam.

"My past," Bobbi said, nodding to the pictures. "I thought they should all be here for the wake."

"Bobbi, the investigation isn't over. I haven't given up yet."

"I have. And to tell you the truth, surrender is oddly liberating. It's funny too. When you accept the future, somehow you see the past more clearly. We plant the seeds early, don't we? We didn't even know it back then. We didn't know anything. But we were so damn sure of ourselves at the time, so invincible, that's the real joke."

I followed her gaze to those faces, frozen in time, careless of wheels being set in motion. I had only a vague suspicion that anything happening so long ago had caused the death of that sweet-faced little girl holding Bobbi's and Lynne's hands. Mostly I thought Bobbi needed to talk and the least I could do was listen. Also, I am cursed with curiosity, and I admit that I was curious.

"Tell me about it, Bobbi," I said.

She handed me a picture I hadn't seen before, actually an old newspaper clipping preserved behind glass, cops in riot gear hauling away students. The headline read: Twenty-Seven Arrested at Berkeley Sit-In.

The faces were too blurred to recognize, but Bobbi pointed and said, "Me and Harvey. We'd been together about six months. We thought we were madly in love, like everybody did back then. Nobody loves like that any more. Maybe it was the demonstrations. We felt so powerful, we really thought we could change the world.''

She picked up the group photo. ''Then we went to Selma, and we met Lynne and Sam. Can you imagine Sam in Selma? He really had me fooled, I think because he fooled himself so well.''

''Lynne and Sam were a couple?''

''No,'' she said. ''They rode down together on the bus.''

''So Sam broke you and Harvey up?''

''Not exactly. There was just this kind of natural split like amoebas separating and reforming. Me and Sam; Harvey and Lynne.''

''Harvey and *Lynne?*'' I said, startled.

''Oh, yes. I was a little jealous at first, I guess. Later it was more that I was envious. Because they were so good together, so right. And I was beginning to see that Sam and I weren't.''

''You were all in Chicago?''

She nodded and put the photos back on the table. ''Sam was in the university there. Harvey and I transferred. We all lived in a co-op, a commune, I guess it was. Sam never really liked it. He liked it less as time went on. Then came the convention in '68. While the rest of us were getting our heads busted, guess what Sam was doing?''

''Enlisting in the Marine Corps,'' I said, recalling Newley's background.

''Bingo,'' Bobbi said.

"That explains you and Sam. What happened with Harvey and Lynne?"

"Time passing, I don't know. Harvey got homesick for California. Lynne wouldn't leave Chicago. She had a child, and no matter how fond Harvey was of Sandy, the little girl wasn't his. Maybe Lynne just didn't love him as much as he loved her. I know it was her decision. Harvey would have done anything to keep them together. But in the end he came home, cut his hair, joined a top-dollar law firm, and married the boss's daughter. Lynne became a school teacher and raised her little girl. I guess I was the only one who clung to the old sixties ideals. Like some kind of disease—and then I infected Sandy..."

She picked up the photo of herself and Lynne and Sandy. "She didn't look very much like her mother. But sometimes there would be a gesture, the way she tilted her head when she listened to you, and for just an instant it was as though Lynne had come back to life."

We were both so drawn into the past that we started in surprise at the sound of the telephone ringing, the noise abnormally loud in the silent room. Bobbi went to answer it, said, "Delilah, it's for you."

Danny was on the line, a note of excitement in his voice. "I don't know if this is important or not, but back in January Sandy called the Sand Dollar Motel in Tustin. The guy who's on the desk tonight was working there at the time, Delilah. He doesn't recognize Sandy's name or remember that she called.

Maybe it's nothing. Maybe she had a friend visiting from out of town and staying there.''

"Maybe," I said. "Do you have an address?"

He gave it to me. Bobbi watched me anxiously and when I hung up, she asked, "What is it?"

"I'm not sure. Just something I need to check out." I came back over, scanned the pictures on her coffee table, and selected the one current photo, a group picture I'd last seen hanging in her office, which contained a good likeness of Sandy among the Slo-Grow volunteers who posed with Bobbi and Harvey.

"Can I take this?" I asked.

"Yes, of course. But can you just tell me—"

"I'll call you," I said. "As soon as I know anything for sure."

It was seven-fifteen now and the traffic had thinned, as light as it gets during daylight hours, which is still nearing overload. To the east, away from the ocean, the sky was still bright, the Santa Ana mountains defined in shades of twilight purple. I made it to the Sand Dollar Motel in half an hour, a record considering freeway construction, plenty of time to speculate about why Sandy had called the motel. I had an idea forming, an ugly possibility, not something I particularly wanted to see take shape and become reality, but something that had to be exposed if it were true.

The motel was two stories of cheap stucco and wood beams badly in need of staining. Located several blocks off the freeway, it probably didn't attract the people off the interstate; maybe it got some spillover from Disneyland. However, I've staked out enough motels to know a nice, discreet rendezvous when I see one. I parked and went inside.

The desk clerk leaned on his elbows on the counter, perusing a tabloid with the weary posture of the terminally bored. Thinning ashy hair had been swept back and gelled in place. His skin was mottled, definitely precancerous. He glanced up, said, "Sorry, we're full," then went back to his scandal sheet.

"I don't want a room," I said. "Just some information."

"Dial 411," he said.

"My calling card." I took out a fifty and laid it on the counter.

He took the bill, a little wary interest in his weasely eyes. "Private cop?"

I nodded.

"I don't need any big-time grief here, you know what I'm saying?"

"No biggie," I said. "Divorce case."

"Still, I could get in a lot of trouble, maybe even lose my job."

I took out another fifty. When he reached for it, I pulled it back. "After you talk to me." I showed him the picture. "You recognize anybody? This may go back as far as last January."

He studied the photo. "Not that far back." He gave me a sly, lewd grin. "I mean that mighta been the first time, but after that—standing reservation. Every Tuesday. Sometimes other days too, but always on Tuesday."

"Who?"

He tapped a long pinkie nail on the glass, confirming the suspicion blooming in the dark corner of my brain. But he was not indicating Sandy.

He was pointing to Harvey Klein.

TWENTY-ONE

Twilight was dying fast, strangled by long, gray ribbons of fog, as I rang the Klein's doorbell. Ellen answered. She looked glassy-eyed and woefully thin and colorless, like some spindly-armed sea creature suddenly brought up to the light.

"Delilah." There was resignation and an unexpected note of dignity in her voice as she said, "Please, come on in."

A fussy, ruffled, lilac-print dress drooped off one pale shoulder and bunched at the belted waist. A pair of beach thongs flopped on her feet as she led the way into the family room.

"Excuse the mess," she said. "I thought I should put a few things away."

Two packing boxes sat in front of the cherrywood cabinets. All the glass doors stood open, and most of the china figurines had been cleared out, not packed neatly away but thrown carelessly into the boxes. Broken bits filled the cartons like bone shards. A delicate Dresden head gleamed up at me from the carpet.

"Is Harvey home?" I asked.

"Not yet. Soon. I have a drink here somewhere—" She spied the glass on an end table and picked it up, leaving a wet whitened ring on the dark wood. "You want something? Help yourself."

"No, thanks," I said. "Let's sit down, Ellen."

She nodded and sat in an armchair, almost primly, ankles together, smoothing her dress over her knees.

"You know, don't you?" She didn't wait for an answer but plunged on. "That first night I met you I could tell you were very bright, and you didn't give up easily. I felt that about you. But then there was the bombing, and I thought if you caught one of those men, well, they were criminals and maybe they would be blamed. I don't know, I think I just told myself that, that I never really believed it. I think I knew all along that it was just a matter of time. How did you find out? Will you tell me that?"

"I checked Sandy's telephone calls," I said. "She called the motel."

A parody of a smile. "The motel—that's how I knew, too, for sure, I mean. No, that's not true. I knew weeks before that, the first time I saw her. It was at some fund-raiser, wildlife or something. I had already guessed there was someone. That's the reason I went. I hate those things, people staring at me and thinking *poor Harvey, married to a lush*. But I went, and I saw her and Harvey together. And then I found out she was Lynne's daughter..."

She downed the rest of her drink. Her hand shook and the glass clattered against her teeth.

"I saw Lynne once, years ago. Harvey's true love. She was visiting Bobbi. Harvey slept with her while she was here. I know he did. He denied it, of course. He denies every little slut he's ever been with, including Bobbi, even though I'm sure he goes back to her. I always know. Always."

She stared down at the ice in her glass as though she was looking into a peephole at the past. "I was a virgin when I married Harvey. Isn't that a joke? He never guessed. I made up a lover, an Irish poet who belonged to the IRA. And I've told Harvey about two affairs I had since—told him in detail, but it was all a lie. I didn't want anybody except Harvey, and he wanted everybody except me.

"He never asked for a divorce, though. Because of our son. Because he didn't love any of the others. But when I saw Sandy I knew this time it would be different, and I was terrified. I tried to tell myself I was wrong. Dear God, I wanted to be wrong. I had to know for sure, so I started following her. I wasn't very good at it. Some days I couldn't manage it at all. But then one evening I followed her to the motel. Harvey was already there. I saw his car. I couldn't move. Couldn't leave. So I sat out there while they..."

She hunched her shoulders as though warding off the memory. Her knuckles whitened on the glass. I remembered the strength of those long bony fingers closing around my arm the first time I had come here. I reached out and took the glass from her. In the silence I heard the distant hum of an electric garage door opening, the sound of a car engine being shut off. Ellen didn't hear it. She was back at the Sand Dollar Motel while her husband made love to another woman.

"When did this happen?" I asked. "Before Sandy was arrested?"

"Yes."

"She might have gone to jail. There was a good case against her." And I certainly should know about that.

"You don't understand. He *loved* her. And her being in trouble—that just drew them closer. I had to do something. So I went to her apartment building to talk to her. She was leaving the parking lot when I drove in. I followed her—to the motel. And I sat outside until I couldn't stand it any more. Then I went somewhere—a bar, but sometimes drinking doesn't help, like today."

I heard Harvey come into the house; I was sure he was walking down the hall as she went on: "I never intended to let Bobbi be convicted. Please believe that. I hate her, but I wouldn't let it go that far. I'm sure I wouldn't."

"Ellen?"

I glanced over. Harvey stood, rooted with horror, in the doorway.

"Ellen," he said. "Don't say another word."

She didn't look surprised to see him. She seemed beyond emotion at this point.

"Oh, Harvey, I have to," she said. "I need to say it."

"No," Harvey said fiercely. "I'm speaking as your attorney now, and I'm telling you to be quiet."

"I saw you together, Harvey, and I went back to the apartment, and I killed her," Ellen said. "I killed her."

ONCE LIEUTENANT BRADY had Ellen's confession, he quickly found corroborating evidence: Ellen's blood-stained clothing, some unidentified fingerprints at the crime scene that matched Ellen's, a witness who saw her drive away from the parking lot.

Harvey stuck by his wife, blaming himself, but then he has reason. He hired the best attorney in the country to defend Ellen. I'm sure they'll plead at least diminished capacity, maybe even temporary insanity.

Bobbi insists she is partially at fault too, saying she not only helped sow those long-ago seeds, she helped to cultivate the bitter crop. "I could have tried to be Ellen's friend; I knew she needed one. I could have done that much."

I tell her we all have our lists: sins of omission and commission strung in our own private rosary. At least, she says, she has no guilt over her relationship to Harvey. Ellen was wrong; they were only friends all these years since Selma.

Certainly Harvey had an affair with Sandy. I'm not sure if the others were real, or if they existed only in Ellen's mind. As you can imagine, I'm not Harvey Klein's confidante of choice. There remains the big question: Did Harvey know his wife murdered Sandy? Or did he merely suspect and suppress the suspicion?

Only Harvey knows, and Harvey isn't talking.

Bobbi did press him for a reason for Sandy's phone calls to both her and to me that last day. He could stonewall me, but he could not refuse Bobbi.

He said Sandy had wanted to call me all along even though he advised her against it. She had liked me when we worked together, and was sure that if only we could talk I would see I had made a terrible mistake about her.

She had become more and more distraught. The day of her death, the day Ellen followed them to the motel, Harvey and Sandy quarreled bitterly. She hated lying to Bobbi and deceiving Ellen. She accused him of loving her only because she was Lynne's daughter, and was too upset to be comforted.

He wanted to cancel his plans and spend the evening with her. Sandy refused. She said she wanted to be alone. He had no idea she had already called me and Bobbi.

Would it have mattered if I had answered Sandy's pleas for help, if I had been in her apartment when Ellen arrived? More than likely Ellen would simply have waited for me to leave, or else she would have left and come back another day. Still, there is the possibility Ellen would have passed that crisis point, gone on home and drunk herself into oblivion, and never worked up her nerve again.

Like I told Bobbi, we all have our lists.

SAM NEWLEY got a little bad press, but his PR agent is hard at work, and I notice a shift in the tone of the media coverage, with poor old Sam becoming the victim of an overzealous employee, guilty only of a trusting nature.

Tony Vero, who totally exonerates his ex-boss, is back at his old job at Newley Development, Inc. Sam has no connection with this, of course, having placed his holdings in trust while he serves the public. Meanwhile Turk, Zack Pellissier, and their Marine connection, Sal Rizzo, are all in federal prison making big rocks into little rocks in a more labor-intensive way.

Bobbi and Sam are still fighting over environmental issues. The County Board and the Planning Commission refused to back down on their approval of a huge development to be built in Laguna Canyon. However, the company that owns the land finally agreed to sell the 2,150 acres to Laguna Beach for the bargain basement price of $78 million dollars.

While everybody celebrated at the Hotel Laguna, the Planning Commission rubberstamped another 2,500 units out in the foothills of the Santa Ana mountains. Meanwhile, somebody took a look at all the parkland Orange County developers were supposed to be setting aside and discovered most of it was vertical and totally unusable except for mountain goats.

My building finally completed repairs on my old office and allowed me to move back in. The insurance company settled, paying off enough to replace my furniture and Danny's computer. Then they quadrupled my premium.

We found Mr. Tilson's highschool sweetheart, Mildred, living a mile away from him, recently widowed from a second husband, with a divorced fortynine-year-old daughter from her first marriage. Mildred wanted nothing to do with Mr. Tilson, saying nursing one old man until he died was quite enough, thank you. However, Mr. Tilson and the daughter fell instantly in love and plan a September wedding. Danny and I are invited. I agreed to go but adamantly refused to be a bridesmaid.

After a lunch with Rita that included two glasses of wine, I had my other ear pierced. Now I have these gold studs that look an awful lot like the ones Zack Pellissier wears.

Business is good, although not as good as it was before I finally had my talk with Erik. When my lease runs out, I'll have to give up the condo for a cheaper apartment, but at least I won't be sleeping in my office.

As for Erik—I kept putting off seeing him, wanting to be absolutely sure of my feelings and being nothing of the kind. I only knew that: A. I had a powerful physical attraction for the man, and B. I was totally nuts if I didn't plow the budding relationship under and sow the ground with salt.

Three weeks went by. Wayne was out of the hospital but not well enough for the full-scale anniversary bash he and Peggy had planned, so they had a small party instead. I went, happy to be part of their celebration, sadly nostalgic, too, because I inevitably thought of Jack.

The party broke up early. Restless, I went for a drive, down the coast, past Corona del Mar and the short stretch of open coastline beyond, past the turnoff to the big house perched high on a hill overlooking the sea.

Just coming into Laguna, I slowed, turned around, and went back. I pulled off the highway at the turnoff and used the car phone to call Erik.

"I'm in the neighborhood," I said. "I thought I'd stop by, but if it's too late—"

"It's never too late," he said.

I wound up through sandstone boulders, yellowing grasses, and scrub oak to a high stone wall camouflaged by pine, juniper, and some kind of dense, thorny bushes. The guard waved me through the opened gate. About a mile further along I parked on the circular drive in front of Erik's sprawling Spanish-style house between the Lamborghini and the Rolls.

An offshore breeze kept the fog out over the Pacific. The warm air smelled of sun-charred sage and flowering chamise. Stars blazed overhead.

The houseman, Ben, let me in and led me to the huge room which I guess is the family room—if such designations apply in a house like that. There were three seven-foot sofas arranged in a U in front of a fireplace. Wide windows were thrown open, giving access to a narrow deck. Erik stood out there, leaning on the sturdy wood railing. Spread out below, all those crowded, overbuilt beehives of coastal cities were just so many diamonds rimming the dark ocean like a great, gaudy necklace.

Erik came inside, saying, "Delilah," and watching me with those blue, blue eyes as though looking for a clue whether to smile or not and deciding against it. Ben went away and left us.

"I'm having a brandy," Erik said. "Join me?"

"No," I said. "Well—maybe just a little."

He brought the drinks and we chose opposite corners of the soft leather sofas.

"I take it this is the talk you promised," Erik said.

"This is it." I took a steadying sip of brandy. "I know you're responsible for a lot of the business that's come my way recently. Believe me, I'm not ungrateful. And the way you took care of me in the hospital—I don't know exactly why you're doing all this—"

"Some detective you are," he said.

I felt my cheeks get warm. "All right, I do know, but dammit, Erik, I don't like it. I don't need a god-father, or a front man, or a puppeteer. So back off."

"That's what you want?"

"I do."

"Okay," he said. "My turn. I want to see you sometime, preferably not in a hospital. Dinner, maybe."

"Erik, this is not a good idea."

"All right, lunch."

Oh, no. No, no. Talk about your two separate worlds. I had nothing in common with this man except, possibly, a love for Monet.

"Delilah? One lunch. We can even go dutch."

Hell.

I intended to say no, I really did.

But what I said was maybe.

A FINE ITALIAN HAND

First Time in Paperback

Eric Wright
An Inspector Charlie Salter Mystery

CHECKOUT TIME

Murder at the seedy Days 'R Done motel is no surprise. But the killing of actor Alec Hunter poses some questions for Toronto Police Inspector Charlie Salter. Namely, what was a nice guy like Alec doing in a place like that?

His death appears to be the work of a fine Italian hand—a Mob-style hit—carried out to settle some gambling debts. Yet the Mob denies the charges. So who was the Italian-looking gentleman who registered for Alec's room at the Days 'R Done?

"Excellent series...humor and insight."
—*New York Times Book Review*

Available in May at your favorite retail stores.

WORLDWIDE LIBRARY®   ITALIAN

WILLFUL INTENT

Gambling had been Muriel's life—it had destroyed her marriage and very nearly her husband's career. Now, in death, Muriel has taken her biggest gamble of all. A deathbed revision of her will leaves everything, including several Las Vegas casinos and a cache of valuable rubies, to ex-husband Lennox Kemp. In doing so, she stiffed some *very* powerful men.

But both the jewels and the second will are missing. So is the nurse who cared for Muriel. Now, with murder and the Mob on his doorstep, English solicitor Lennox Kemp gets a taste of the action—Nevada-style.

"Meek never fails to be engaging...."
—*Cleveland Plain Dealer*

TOUCH & GO

M.R.D. MEEK

A Lennox Kemp Mystery

First Time in Paperback

Available in June at your favorite retail stores.

TOUCH